The world went still for Celia. All of it.

Including her boss. He was sitting in his black leather chair at the huge glass-topped table that served as his desk, in front of a wall that was also a window. Beyond lay Las Vegas, the magical, impossible city in the desert.

But it wasn't Las Vegas Celia was staring at.

It was Aaron Bravo.

All of him, every last detail, was suddenly achingly clear.

Tall. Broad-shouldered. Lean. That face, with a cleft in the strong chin. His gorgeous designer suit.

In that frozen moment, as his image seared itself into her brain, it hit Celia...

She loved her boss!

Available in August 2003 from Silhouette Special Edition

His Executive Sweetheart

CHRISTINE RIMMER

SILHOUETTE®
SPECIAL EDITION™

First published in Great Britain 2003
Silhouette Books, Eton House, 18-24 Paradise Road,
Richmond, Surrey TW9 1SR

© Christine Rimmer 2002

ISBN 0 373 24485 1

23-0803

Printed and bound in Spain
by Litografia Rosés S.A., Barcelona

For my own sons,
Matt and Jess,
with all my love.

CHRISTINE RIMMER

came to her profession the long way around. Before
settling down to write about the magic of romance,
she'd been an actress, a sales clerk, a janitor, a model, a
phone sales representative, a teacher, a waitress, a
playwright and an office manager. She insists she
never had a problem keeping a job—she was merely
gaining 'life experience' for her future as a novelist.
Christine is grateful not only for the joy she finds in
writing, but for what waits when the day's work is
through: a man she loves, who loves her right back, and
the privilege of watching their children grow and
change day to day. She lives with her family in
Oklahoma, USA.

SILHOUETTE® SPECIAL EDITION™

is proud to present the all-new trilogy continuing the Bravo family saga from

CHRISTINE RIMMER

THE SONS OF CAITLIN BRAVO

**Aaron, Cade and Will—
can any woman tame them?**

HIS EXECUTIVE SWEETHEART
August 2003

MERCURY RISING
October 2003

SCROOGE AND THE SINGLE GIRL
December 2003

Chapter One

It happened on Valentine's Day.

Which was just a coincidence, really. An irony. An accident of timing that made the whole thing all the more pitiful, somehow.

It was Valentine's Day and it was a Wednesday, at 9:15 a.m. in the Executive Tower of High Sierra Resort and Casino. Celia Tuttle was taking a memo—well, getting e-mail instructions, really. Her boss, Aaron Bravo, never actually composed the in-office e-mails he sent out to the managers and senior vice presidents who labored under him. He told Celia what he wanted to get across. As his executive secretary/personal assistant it was her job to put appropriate wording to his commands.

Her boss said, "We've got to do something about the line for that damn raft ride...."

Celia smiled to herself as she scribbled on her note-pad. High Sierra contained its own river, complete with rushing rapids and a whitewater raft ride. The ride was incredibly popular—so much so that the long lines of customers waiting their turn sometimes got in the way of casino traffic. At High Sierra, as in any gaming establishment worthy of its name, *nothing* was allowed to get in the way of casino traffic. They called it a resort and casino, but everyone knew it was really the other way around.

"Send an e-mail to Hickock Drake." Hickock was a senior vice president. "Tell him to sit on Carter Biles." Carter Biles was Director of Rides and Attractions. "It's too many people standing around in a line when they ought to be at the tables or playing the slots. Carter should know that. Up the price on the ride till no one will pay it. Shut the damn thing down. Whatever. The line is in the way and I want it out of there."

It happened right then. Celia looked up from her legal pad, still smiling a little at the whole idea of an amusement park ride upstaging the mighty gaming tables. Aaron said, "And before the meeting with the planning commission, I need you to check with…"

She didn't really catch the rest of it because everything seemed to spin to a stop. It was something out of a sci-fi movie, the kind where the world freezes in place and one woman is left walking and talking in the usual way while trying to deal with the fact that everyone she knows is suddenly a statue.

Yes. The world went still. All of it.

Including Aaron. He was sitting in his glove-soft

black leather chair at the huge glass-topped chrome-legged table that served as his desk, in front of a wall that was also a window. Behind him and below him lay the Las Vegas Strip, a modern-day Mecca, a land of turrets and towers, sphinxes and circus tents. Beyond the strip stretched the glittering sprawl of the magical, impossible city in the desert.

But it wasn't the city of Las Vegas Celia Tuttle was staring at.

It was Aaron.

And all of him, every last physical detail, was suddenly achingly clear.

Tall, she thought, as if that was news. Broad-shouldered. Lean. A face that wasn't quite handsome. Long and angular, that face, with a cleft in the strong chin. And a nose that would have been bladelike, had it not been broken at some point in his checkered past.

He wore a gorgeous lightweight designer suit. Navy, chalk stripe. A lustrous silk shirt. A paisley tie in plum and indigo. The suit had been handmade by his ultra-exclusive Manhattan tailor, everything in the best fabrics.

He had his computer in front of him, a little to the side. He'd been clicking the mouse as he spoke, his blue gaze mostly on the screen, but now and then flicking her way. What did he see on the screen? Probably his e-mail—to which Celia would end up composing the replies.

Or could be he was looking over some marketing or design prospectus. Aaron rarely did just one thing at a time. He was a driven man. Only thirty-four and part owner and CEO of one of Las Vegas's top super-casinos. Multi-tasking was not a concept to him. It was the way he lived his life.

In that frozen moment, as his image seared itself into her brain, it hit her.

She loved him.

Somehow, the thought of that, the *admission* of that, brought the world to life again.

She heard a siren, out there somewhere in the vast city beyond the window wall. And far out over the desert, just above the rim of the mountains, a silver jet streaked by, leaving a white trail in its wake.

And in the huge office room, Aaron was clicking his mouse again, frowning at the computer screen, giving her instructions at the same time.

Not that she was capable, right at that second, of making sense of anything he said to her. But it was okay—at least the part about not really hearing him. She had her mini-recorder going, as she always did for their morning meetings, providing a backup in case her own notes fell short. She would need it big-time later, since right now, incoming information was not getting through in any rational form. She felt…so strange. Disordered. Confused. Embarrassed. In complete emotional disarray.

All she could think was, *How can this be?*

She and Aaron Bravo enjoyed a strictly professional relationship. The only time he really noticed her was when she wasn't getting her job done— which, at least in the past two and a half years or so, was pretty much never.

It had always been just fine with Celia that her boss didn't notice her. He was a fair boss. Yes, he worked her very hard; she rarely got a weekend off. But he also paid her well. She had a great benefits package and points in the company.

And she loved her job.

But she didn't love her boss. Or at least, she hadn't until about forty seconds ago.

Then again, maybe she just hadn't realized it until now. Maybe it had been happening for a long time, coming on slowly, like a nagging cold that never quite catches hold for weeks and weeks and then—bang— in a flash it hits you. You've got pneumonia and you've got it bad.

Oh—she held back a small, anguished groan—this was ridiculous.

Over time, it was true, she'd grown…rather fond of Aaron Bravo. He was really a much nicer person than a lot of people thought. And all those rumors about junk bonds and Wise Guy connections? Patently untrue.

Celia was certain of that now, after three years of working for him. He wasn't a shady character at all, but an honest businessman with lady luck in his corner. He'd made a few very risky investments—in computer games and real estate. He'd seen those investments pay off in a major way and put the profits into carving out a niche for himself in the gaming industry.

Frankly, Celia had been a little nervous when she first took the job with him. After all, they'd grown up just blocks from each other, up north in New Venice—yes, named after that famous city in Italy, though New Venice, Nevada, was pronounced *Noo-*

vuneece, with the accent over the ''neece.'' It was nowhere near the sea and it didn't have a single canal. Instead, it lay tucked against the eastern slopes of the Sierras in the beautiful Comstock Valley not far from Lake Tahoe.

Celia was eight years younger than Aaron, but she'd grown up on the stories of the notorious Caitlin Bravo and her three wild boys—each of whom, by the way, was now doing nothing short of spectacularly in his chosen field.

And yes, all right. Maybe there *was* an air of danger, of risk, of something not quite safe, about Aaron Bravo. But that, Celia had decided, was part of his charm. He was the kind of man you didn't challenge unless you were willing to fight to the brutal end.

He was tough. And uncompromising. He had to be. But at the core, she knew him as a fair man, and essentially kind.

And she was proud—yes, she was—to work for him. She had, at least in the past couple of years, felt *warmly* toward him.

But love?

How could this be happening?

''Celia? Are you all right?''

Celia blinked. Aaron was staring at her—*noticing* her—because she was very obviously *not* doing her job.

She checked her recorder—working fine, thank God—and straightened her shoulders. ''Uh. Yes. Okay. Really. I am.''

''You're certain? You look a little—''

"Honestly Aaron, there's nothing. I'm okay." Yes, it was an outright lie. But what else could she say?

Right then, the phone in his pocket rang.

Saved by the bell, she thought with an inward sigh of relief.

Aaron pulled out the ringing phone, flipped it open, spoke a few sentences into it, swung it shut and put it away.

Celia cleared her throat and poised her pen. "Now. Where were we?"

They got back to work.

But from that frozen moment on, for Celia Tuttle, nothing was the same.

The hours that followed were pure misery. Insanely, now that she'd acknowledged its existence, the longing she felt seemed to grow stronger minute by minute. It hurt, just being near him, going over the rest of the calendar with him—and having him not once look up and make eye contact.

Now, really, why should that bother her? It certainly never had before.

But all of a sudden she was…so hungry for any kind of contact.

And yet, when she got contact, it hurt almost as much as having none at all.

Take, for instance, his hand brushing hers….

It happened all the time, though she'd hardly noticed it before. He would ask for something—an update, a file, a letter, a cup of coffee, black—and she would see he got it. And if she had to come near him to deliver it, he would touch the back of her hand or maybe her wrist or her forearm. It would be just a breath of a touch, a little thank-you, without words. Something that was so small, so unremarkable, that she hardly recalled it once it had happened.

Well, until *now* she'd hardly recalled it.

"Did the estimates come in on the South Tower remodel?" At High Sierra, the hotel rooms and the rides, the casino and the showrooms, were in a constant cycle of remodeling. Things had to stay fresh to lure in the crowds.

She told him where to look for it.

"It's not coming up."

She put down her legal pad and went around behind him where she had a view of the screen.

Oh, Lord. He did smell good. So clean and fresh and...male. She'd always liked the aftershave he used. She liked his hair, short but kind of wavy, a dark brown that sometimes, in the right light, still managed to show glints of gold. And the shape of his ears...

He glanced back at her, one eyebrow lifted.

Her heart lurched in her chest and she ordered her face not to flush beet-red. "Hmm," she said. "Let's see..." She reached for the mouse. Two clicks and the information he wanted appeared.

"Good. Thanks."

As she withdrew her hand, he touched the back of it—just that quick brush of warm acknowledgement. She almost gasped, but somehow held back the sound. Her skin flamed where his fingers had grazed it—so lightly, so fleetingly. For Aaron, she knew, the touch was the next thing to a subconscious act. He did it and forgot it.

Not for Celia. Not anymore. Suddenly, his slightest touch seared her to her very soul.

She made herself cross back around the desk and return to her chair. She picked up her legal pad again and waited for him to go on.

For the next ten minutes, the situation was almost bearable. They got through his calendar for the day, the rest of the memos and letters he would be wanting, the reports he needed her to get in hard copy and bind for the next managers' meeting.

They were winding things up when he added off-handedly, "And would you get something nice for Jennifer? Since it *is* Valentine's Day…"

It felt like a knife straight through the heart, when he said that. *Get something nice for Jennifer*….

Jennifer Tartaglia had a featured role in the hit review, *Gold Dust Follies,* playing nightly in High Sierra's Excelsior Theatre. Jennifer was Cuban and Italian, drop-them-in-their-tracks gorgeous—and a very nice person, as well. The first time the showgirl had visited the office tower, she'd made it a point to say hi to Aaron's secretary.

"Hello, so nice to meet you." Jennifer had stuck out her hand and beamed a radiant smile. "I hear you take fine care of Aaron."

They shook hands. "I do my best."

"You *are* the best. He tells me so." Still smiling that wide, friendly, breathtaking smile, Jennifer tossed her honey-blond mane of hair and turned to walk away. Celia had found herself staring. The rear view of Jennifer Tartaglia—especially in motion—was something to see.

But so what if no woman had a right to look that good? Celia *liked* Jennifer. She considered Jennifer a good person who was, no doubt, very good to Aaron—not that the relationship was anything truly serious. It never was, with Aaron.

Aaron Bravo…enjoyed women, and a man in his position had his pick of some of the most beautiful, talented and seductive women in the world. But none of them, at least in the years Celia had worked for him, had lasted. Aaron always gave them diamonds—a bracelet or a necklace—at the end. Eventually, Celia knew, she'd be buying diamonds for Jennifer.

He really was married to his work. And so busy he thought nothing of asking his assistant to buy his girlfriend thoughtful gifts and expensive trinkets whenever the occasion arose—like for Valentine's Day.

"Something nice for Jennifer," Celia parroted in the voice of a dazed windup doll.

He was frowning again. "Are you *certain* there's nothing wrong?"

"I am. Positive. No problem. Sincerely."

An hour later, Celia left High Sierra to get Jennifer that gift. She found a heart-shaped ruby-encrusted pin in one of the elite little boutiques at Caesar's Forum Shops. High Sierra had its own series of exclusive shops, the Gold Exchange, in the central court between the casino and the 3,000-room hotel. But Celia never shopped in-house for gifts "from" the boss. To her, it seemed more appropriate, more *personal,* if she went outside Aaron's realm of influence to get little treasures for his lady friends.

And hey, wasn't that great reasoning? she found herself thinking, now unrequited love was souring her attitude. He wasn't even choosing the gifts. How personal could they be?

She bought the pin, brought it back to High Sierra and showed it to him, so that he'd know what lovely little trinket Jennifer was getting from him.

"Great, Celia. She'll love it."

Tears tightened her throat as she wrapped up that ruby heart. But she didn't cry. She swallowed those tears down.

By then, it had been a mere six hours since she'd realized she was in love with him. She couldn't afford to start blubbering like a baby from day one, now could she? And maybe, she couldn't help thinking as she expertly tied the red satin ribbon, this sudden, overwhelming and inconvenient passion would just…burn itself out. Soon.

Oh, yes. Please God. Let it be over soon….

But her prayer was not answered, at least not in the next week. The days went by and the longing didn't fade.

She managed, somehow, never to cry over it, in spite of how close she'd come that first day. And he never guessed. She was sure of it. She took a kind of bleak pride in that, in the fact that he didn't know she was hopelessly, utterly gone on him.

Yes, sometimes he gave her a faintly puzzled look. As if he knew something wasn't quite right with her. But she did her job and she did it well and after that first day, he never asked again what might be wrong with her.

Fresh torments abounded.

Simple things. Everyday things. Like his brushing touch, they were things that had meant next to nothing before. Things like following him around the executive suite taking last-minute instructions before he met his managers for lunch—as he stripped to the waist and changed into a fresh shirt.

She tried not to stare at his muscled back and lean, hard arms, not to let herself imagine what it would be like if he held out those arms to her, if he gathered her close against that broad chest, if he lowered that wonderful mouth to cover hers....

It was awful. She had seen him change his shirt fifty times, at least. She'd never thought of a fresh shirt as a new form of torture. Until now.

Really, their lives were so...intertwined. They both lived where they worked. Aaron had a penthouse suite. Celia's rooms were smaller, of course, and several floors below his.

She'd always loved that, living on-site. She loved the glamour and excitement of her life at High Sierra. In many ways, the resort was its own city. A person could eat, sleep, shop, work and play there and never have to leave. The party went on 24/7, as the tired saying went.

Celia was far from a party animal. But working for Aaron, she felt as if some of the gold dust and glitter rubbed off on her. Growing up, she'd been just a little bit shy, and not all that popular—not unattractive, really, but a long way from gorgeous. She came from a big family, the fourth child of six. Her parents were good parents, but a little distracted. There were so many vying for their attention. She felt closer to her two best friends, Jane Elliott and Jillian Diamond, than she did to her own brothers and sisters.

She'd earned an accounting degree from Cal State Sacramento and worked for a Sacramento CPA firm before she stumbled on a job as secretary/assistant to one of the firm's clients, a local morning talk-show host.

Celia adored that job. It suited her perfectly. She needed to be organized and businesslike—and she also needed to be ready for anything. She handled correspondence and personal bookkeeping, as well as shopping and spur-of-the-moment dinner parties. Her duties were rarely the same from one day to the next.

The talk-show host had done a segment on High Sierra. Aaron had agreed to a brief interview. And then he'd been there, behind the scenes, for the rest of the shoot. And he'd remembered the girl from his hometown.

Two months later, the talk-show host got another show—in Philadelphia. Celia could have gone, too. But she decided against the move.

Aaron's human resources people had contacted her. She flew to Vegas to see him and he hired her on the spot.

"You're just what I'm looking for, Celia," he had said. "Efficient. Cool-headed. Low key. Smart. And someone from home, too. I like that. I really do."

It had been a successful working relationship pretty much from the first—impersonally intimate, was how Celia always thought of it. She was a true "office wife" and that was fine with her. She was good at what she did, she enjoyed the work and her boss knew her value. She'd had a number of raises since she'd started at High Sierra. Now, she was making twice what she'd made in the beginning. She'd been happy with the talk-show host, but she'd really come into her own since she became Aaron's assistant. Now, instead of shy, she saw herself as reserved. Serene. Unruffled.

She was that calm place in the eye of any storm that brewed up at High Sierra. Aaron counted on her to keep his calendar in order, his letters typed and his personal affairs running smoothly. And she did just that, with skill and panache. She was a happy, successful career woman—until she had to go and fall for the boss and ruin everything.

Now, it was all changed. Now, it was the agony and the ecstasy and Celia Tuttle was living it. Everything about being near him excited her—and wounded her to the core.

By the fourth day, she felt just desperate enough to consider telling him of her feelings.

But what for? To make it all the worse? Make her humiliation complete? After all, if he *were* interested, even minimally, wouldn't he have given her some hint, some *clue,* by now?

She told him nothing.

By the sixth day, she found herself contemplating the impossible: giving notice. Less than a week since she'd fallen for the boss. And she'd almost forgotten how much she used to love her job.

Now, work seemed more like torture. A place where she suffered constantly in the company of her heart's desire—and he was totally oblivious to her as anything but his very efficient gal Friday.

Maybe she *should* quit.

But she didn't. She did nothing, just tried to get through each day. Just reminded herself that it really hadn't been all that long since V-day—yes, that was how she had started to think of it. As V-day, the day her whole world went haywire.

She hoped, fervently, that things would get better, somehow.

The seventh day passed.

Then, on the eighth day, Celia got a call from her friend Jane in New Venice.

It was after midnight. Celia had just let herself into her rooms. A group of Japanese businessmen had arrived that afternoon. High rollers, important ones. The kind who thought nothing of dropping a million a night at High Sierra's gaming tables. The kind known affectionately in the industry as *whales*.

Aaron had joined these particular whales for their comped gourmet dinner in the Placer Room. He'd asked Celia to be there, too. She'd been in what she thought of as "fetch-and-carry mode." If there was anything he needed that, for some reason, the wait staff or immediately available hotel personnel couldn't handle, Celia was right there, to see he got it and got it fast.

The phone was ringing when she entered her rooms. She rushed to answer it.

And she heard her dear friend's voice complaining, "Don't you ever return your calls?"

Celia scrunched the phone between her shoulder and her ear and slid her thumb under the back strap of her black evening sandal. "Sorry." She slipped the shoe off with a sigh of relief, then got rid of the other one and dropped to the couch. "It's been a zoo."

"That's what you always say."

"Well, it's always a zoo."

"But you love it."

In her mind's eye, she saw Aaron. "That's right," she said bleakly. "I do."

"Okay, what's wrong?"

"Not a thing."

"You said that too fast."

"Jane. I love my job. It's not news." *Too bad I also love my boss—who does not love me.* "What's up?"

"You're sure you're all right?"

"Uh-huh. What's up?"

Jane hesitated. Celia could just see her, sitting up in her four-poster bed in the wonderful Queen Anne Victorian she'd inherited from her beloved Aunt Sophie. She'd be braced against the headboard, pillows propped at her back, her wildly curling almost-black hair tamed, more or less, into a single braid. And she'd have a frown between her dark brows as she considered whether to get to why she'd called—or pursue Celia's sudden strange attitude toward her job.

Finally, she said, "Come home. This weekend."

Celia leaned back against the couch cushions and stared up at the recessed ceiling lights. "I can't. You know I can't."

Jane made a humphing sound. "I don't know any

such thing. You work too hard. You never take a break.''

"It's Thursday. Home is five hundred miles away."

"That's why they invented airplanes. I'll pick you up in Reno tomorrow, just name the time."

"Oh, Jane…"

"There will be wine. And a crackling fire in the fireplace. The valley is beautiful. We had snow, just enough to give us that picture-postcard effect. But there's none in the forecast, so getting here will be no problem. And Jilly's coming."

Jillian Diamond, Celia's other best friend, lived in Sacramento now and got home almost as rarely as Celia did.

"Also, I'm cooking." Jane was an excellent cook. "Come on, Ceil. It's been way too long. You know it has. At some point, you just have to put work aside for a day or two and come and see your old friends."

Celia gathered her legs up to the side and switched the phone to her other ear. Why not? She thought. She hadn't had a weekend to herself in months. And she could certainly use a break right about now. Yes. A change of scenery, a little time away from the object of her hopeless desire—and everything connected with him.

"Celia Louise?"

"I'm here—and I'm coming."

Jane let out short whoop of glee. "You are? You're serious?"

"I'll get a flight right now, then e-mail you my

flight schedule. But don't worry about picking me up.''

''I don't mind.''

''Forget about it. I'll rent a car, no problem.''

''I'm holding you to this,'' Jane said in a scolding tone. ''You won't be allowed to back out this time.''

''Don't worry. I'll be there. Tomorrow afternoon. Expect me.''

''I will.''

Celia hung up and ran upstairs to her loft office nook, where she scheduled a flight online—quickly, before she could start thinking of all the ways her unexpected absence might be inconvenient for Aaron. She sent Jane a copy of her itinerary.

Jane e-mailed her right back: *Since you're driving yourself, I'll go ahead and stay at the store until six.*

Jane owned and operated a bookstore, the Silver Unicorn, in the heart of New Venice, right on Main Street. It was next door to the Highgrade, the café/saloon/gift shop that Caitlin Bravo, Aaron's mother, had owned and run for over thirty years.

Celia stared at the computer screen, remembering....

Aaron and his brothers used to hang around on Main Street. They all three worked on and off at the Highgrade—in the gift shop or in the café, where they bussed tables or even flipped burgers on the grill. But they were a volatile family. People in town said those boys needed the influence of a steady father figure and that was something they would never get with Caitlin Bravo for a mother.

They were always getting into trouble, or just plain

not showing up when it was time to go to work. Caitlin would pitch a fit and fire them. Then they'd end up hanging out on the street with the other wild kids in town—until they got into some mischief or other. Then Caitlin would yell at them and put them to work again.

Once, when she was eight, Celia had borrowed her big sister's bike and ridden it over to Main Street. It was twenty-six inches of bike, with thin racing wheels, and she'd borrowed it without getting Annie's permission. But she figured she wouldn't get in trouble. Annie was over at the high school, at cheerleading practice. By the time Annie got home, the bike would be back on the side porch where she'd left it.

It was a stretch for Celia's eight-year-old legs to reach the pedals and she kind of wobbled when she rode it. She had wobbled onto Main Street—and lost control right in front of the Highgrade. The bike went down, Celia with it, scraping her knees and palms on the asphalt of the street as she tried to block the fall.

Her legs were all tangled up in the pedals. She grunted and struggled and tried to get free. But it wasn't working and she was getting more and more frustrated. She was on the verge of forgetting all about her eight-year-old dignity, just about to start bawling like a baby in sheer misery.

But then a pair of dusty boots appeared on the street about three feet from where she lay in a clumsy tangle. She looked up two long, strong legs encased in faded jeans, past a black T-shirt, into the face of the oldest of those bad Bravo boys, Aaron.

He knelt at her side. "Hey. You okay?"

She didn't know what to say to him. She pressed her lips together and glared to show him that she wasn't scared of him and she wasn't going to cry.

He said, "Here. I'll help you." He gently took her beneath the arms and slid her out from under the bike. She was on her feet before she had time to shout at him to let go of her.

He stood her up and then he knelt again, just long enough to right the bike. "There you go."

Her tongue felt like a slab of wood in her mouth. She knew if she tried to answer, some strange, ugly sound would be all that came out. She managed a nod.

He frowned at her. "You sure you're all right?"

She nodded again.

"Maybe you should get a smaller bike...."

The cursor on her computer screen blinked at her. Celia ordered her mind back to the present and read the rest of Jane's note. *Key where it always is. Jane.*

She typed, *Can't wait. See you.* And sent it off.

Then she shut down the computer and went to bed. She didn't sleep all that well. She kept obsessing over what Aaron might say when she told him she had to be at the airport at four.

He did depend on her. He could be angry that she was leaving for two days on such short notice. He often needed her on the weekends.

Well, if he said he needed her, she'd just have to cancel, she'd have to call Jane and—

Celia sat up in bed. "Oh, what is the matter with me?"

She flopped back down.

Of course, she wouldn't cancel. She'd promised her dear friend she'd be there, and she would not break her word.

And what right did Aaron have to be angry? She'd worked weekend after weekend and never complained.

She was going. And that was it. No matter what Aaron said.

Chapter Two

As it turned out, she needn't have stayed awake stewing all night.

Aaron was staring at his computer screen when she mentioned her plans. "Hmm," he said. "You'll be here until four?"

"Well, I'd have to leave by three or so."

"Three..." He frowned at the screen, punched a few keys, then added, "No problem. God knows you deserve a little time to yourself. Your parents all right?"

"I'm not going to visit them. They don't live there anymore. None of my family lives there anymore. Remember I told you my folks moved to Phoenix last year?"

"Yeah, that's right. You did." He typed in a few

more commands. She knew that he hadn't really heard her. The next time she went home, he'd be telling her to enjoy her visit with her parents.

"I'll be staying with my friend, Jane Elliott," she volunteered brightly—as if he really cared or needed to know.

"Jane. The mayor's daughter, right?"

The Elliotts were the closest thing New Venice had to an aristocracy. Jane's father was a judge, like his father before him.

"No," Celia said. "It's Jane's uncle, J.T., who's the mayor."

A half smile lifted one side of that wonderful, sculpted mouth of his—though he never took his eyes off his computer screen. "J. T. Elliott. Her *uncle*. Got it."

J. T. Elliott had once been the county sheriff. If Celia remembered right, he'd locked Aaron up in his jail more than once in the distant past. Or if not Aaron, then surely his baby brother, Cade, who was the wildest of the three bad Bravo boys.

"So it's all right, then, if I go?"

"Of course. Have a good time."

Somehow, it felt worse that he didn't seem to care she was leaving than if he'd been a jerk and demanded she cancel her plans and remain at his beck and call the whole weekend through.

Celia told herself to snap out of it. She was getting what she'd asked for and she would take it and be happy about it.

She worked until two-thirty and she was on that plane, flying to Reno, by a little after five that evening.

It was the second bottle of Chianti that did it. Celia probably could have kept her mouth shut if they'd stuck with just one.

But it was such a perfect evening. The three of them—friends since the first day of kindergarten, bosom buddies all through high school—together again, like in the old days.

Jane had cooked. Italian. Something with angel-hair pasta and lots of garlic and sun-dried tomatoes. After the meal, the three of them kicked off their shoes and gathered around the big fireplace in the front parlor. Jane had the stereo on low, set to Random, playing a mix of everything from Tony Bennett to Natalie Imbruglia.

Jillian raised her glass. ''Triple Threat.'' That was the three of them, the Triple Threat. Though, of course, they really hadn't been much of a threat to anyone.

They were three nice girls from a small town, girls who studied hard in school and got good grades and didn't get breasts as early as they would have liked— well, not Celia and Jillian, anyway. At the age of twelve, Jane had suddenly sprouted a pair of breasts that instantly became the envy of even the most popular girls at Mark Twain Middle School, eighth-graders included.

They were all well behaved. Yep. Jane and Jillian and Celia were good girls to the core, their transgressions so minor they generally went unremarked. They only dreamed of rebellions—at least until their senior year, when Jane ran off to Reno and married Rusty Jenkins.

That had been a real mess, Jane's marriage to Rusty. He was trouble, capital T, that Rusty. He'd ended up getting himself killed three years later. Jane had scrupulously avoided all forms of rebellion ever since.

Jillian had tried marriage, too, when she was twenty-two. Her husband had a problem with monogamy—a problem he never bothered to reveal before the wedding. But it turned out that Benny Simmerson found being faithful way too limiting. That marriage had lasted a little over a year.

"Triple Threat," echoed Jane. Celia said it, too. The three of them clinked glasses and drank.

Jillian grabbed a sapphire-blue chenille pillow from the end of the couch, propped it against the front of an easy chair and used it for a backrest. "So, how's construction going next door?"

About six months ago, Cade Bravo had bought the house next to Jane's. Since then, he'd been remodeling it.

Jane sipped more wine. "Who knows? He'll probably never move in."

"Why do you say that?" prodded Jillian. "What? He's never there?"

"He's there. Now and then. You can see he's got the new roof on and the exterior painted. And I do hear hammering inside every once in a while. I'd say construction is moving along."

"The question," said Jillian, "is *why?* Why buy a

house here? I heard he's got a huge place in Vegas. And one in Tahoe, too, right? What's New Venice got to offer that he can't get in Vegas or Tahoe? And why an old house? Cade Bravo is not the fixer-upper type."

"A hungering for the home he never really had?" Jane suggested. "A yearning for a simpler, gentler kind of life?"

Jillian pretended to choke on her wine. "Oh, right. Cade Bravo. Not."

Jane shrugged. "It's only a guess."

"And speaking of Bravos..." Jillian wiggled her eyebrows. "Rumor has it Caitlin's got a new boyfriend."

"Could be," said Jane.

Jillian giggled, a very naughty sound. "Janey. Come on. Who is he? What's he like?"

"Hans is his name. I've seen him tooling around town in that black Trans Am of Caitlin's." Caitlin had owned the Trans Am for as long as Celia could remember. She kept it in perfect condition. It looked just like the one Burt Reynolds drove in that old seventies classic, *Smokey and the Bandit.* Jane added, "Hans has come in the bookstore once or twice."

"And...?"

"Sounds like Arnold Schwarzenegger. Looks like him, too. At least from the neck down. Arnold meets Fabio. Remember Fabio? Long blond hair, major muscles. That's Hans. Buys books on body culture and vitamin therapy."

"A health nut."

"Could be."

"How old?"

Jane tried to look disapproving. "Honestly, Jilly. You're practically salivating."

Jillian let out a long, crowing laugh. "Boytoy! Admit it. I've got it right."

Jane shrugged. "She always did like them young."

"And vigorous." Jillian giggled some more.

Jane gathered her legs up under her and stood. "I'll get that other bottle."

Celia looked down into her almost-empty glass, thinking of Aaron again, feeling disgustingly sorry for herself. There was no escape, really, from thinking of Aaron. Reminders were everywhere. She worked for him, they came from the same hometown where everybody loved nothing so much as to gossip about his mother. And now his brother was moving in next door to her best friend....

Jillian said, "What's with you, Celia Louise?"

Celia looked up from her wine glass. "Huh?"

"I said, what's with you?"

She made an effort to sit straighter and tried to sound perky. "Oh, nothing much. Working, as always."

Jillian looked at her sideways. "No. I mean right this minute. Tonight. You've been too quiet."

"A person can't be quiet?"

"Depends on the *kind* of quiet. Tonight you are...suspiciously quiet. Something's up with you."

"You think so?"

"I do."

Celia put on a frown, as if she were giving the whole idea of something being "up" with her serious thought. Then she shrugged and shook her head. "No. Honestly. Just...enjoying being here."

"Oh, you liar," said Jillian.

Jane came back with the fat, raffia-wrapped bottle. "She said there's nothing bothering her, am I right?"

"You are," said Jillian.

There's something," Jane said. "But she isn't telling."

Both Jane and Jillian looked at Celia, their faces expectant, waiting for her to come clean and tell them what was on her mind. She kept her mouth shut.

Finally, Jane shrugged. "More of this nice, rustic Chianti, anyone?"

Celia and Jillian held out their glasses and Jane filled them. They all sat back and stared at the fire for a minute or two while Tony Bennett sang about leaving his heart in San Francisco.

"Good a place as any," Jane said softly.

Jillian sighed.

Celia drank more wine. She grabbed a couple of pillows of her own, propped them against the wall between the fireplace and the side door that led out to Jane's wraparound porch and leaned back, getting comfortable.

"So, how's the book biz?" Jillian tipped her glass at Jane.

"The book biz is not bad. Not bad at all." Jane's dark eyes shone with satisfaction as she talked about her store. "Events," she said. "They really bring in the customers. Events. Activities." Not a week went by that she didn't have some author or other in to answer questions and sign books. "I still have my

Children's Story Hour, Saturdays at ten and Thursday nights at seven.'' And then there were the reading groups. She offered the store as a place to hold them. ''So far, I've got four different groups meeting at the Silver Unicorn at various times during the week. Now and then I've been doing a kind of café evening on a weekend night, with a harpist or a guitar player, that sort of thing. They can have coffee and tea and scones and biscotti. They can read the books while they enjoy the music. Folks love it. I'm building my customer base just fine. I get the tourists in the summer months and during the winter, the locals have started thinking of the store as a gathering place.''

Jillian said, ''Speaking of speakers, how 'bout me? I am an author now, after all—more or less, anyway.''

Jane grinned. ''I thought you'd never ask. Maybe we could set something up for next month. You could talk about the column. Give a few helpful hints on wardrobe basics, tell them what items they just can't be without this year.''

Jillian had her own business, Image by Jillian. She showed executives and minor celebrities how to spruce up their wardrobes; she gave makeovers and seminars on dressing Business Casual. She also wrote an advice column, ''Ask Jillian,'' for the *Sacramento Press-Telegram.*

Celia sipped her wine, growing dangerously mushy and sentimental as she listened to her two oldest and dearest friends talking shop. Really, she *was* glad she had come. It was just what she'd needed, to be sitting here by the fire at Jane's, getting plotzed on Chianti.

And also, *I need truth,* she thought, with a sudden

burst of semi-inebriated insight. *Truth.* Oh, yes. I need it. I do. I need to *share* the truth with someone—and who better than my two best friends in all the world?

So she said, "Well, the truth is, I'm in love with Aaron Bravo."

Chapter Three

Jillian, who'd been making a point about flirty reversible bias-cut skirts in light, floaty fabrics, shut her mouth right in the middle of a sentence. Jane turned to Celia and stared.

Celia took another large sip of wine.

"Get *out*," said Jillian, after several seconds of stunned silence. A wild laugh escaped her, but she cut it off by clapping her hand over her mouth. Finally, she whispered, "You're serious."

"I am. I love him." Celia looked into her glass again and wrinkled her nose. "Maybe I'll become a drunk. Drown my sorrows…"

Jane reached out and snared the glass.

"Hey," Celia protested, but without much heat.

Jane scooted over and set the glass on the coffee

table, then scooted back to the nest of pillows she'd made for herself on the pretty lapis-blue hand-woven rug in front of the fire.

Jillian asked, "Does he know?"

Oh, no, Celia thought. *Here come those pesky tears again....*

Well, she wasn't having any of them. She jumped to her feet and looked down at her friends. She swallowed. Twice. Finally, her throat loosened up enough that she could tell them, "He hasn't got a clue."

"Oh, honey," cried Jillian. She reached up her arms. So did Jane.

With a tiny sob, Celia toppled toward her friends. They embraced. It felt really good, really comforting.

So much so that she didn't end up bawling like a baby after all.

Once they'd shared a good, long hug, Jane gave Celia back her wineglass. "But don't get too crazy with that."

"I won't. I promise. This is all I'll have. I was only joking about becoming a drunk."

"Good." Jane folded her legs lotus-style and adjusted her long, soft skirt over them. "So. All right. Talk to us. Tell us everything."

Celia explained about V-day.

"Wait a minute," Jillian said. "So you're saying, all this time you've been working for him and you were—what—*fond* of him and nothing more?"

"Oh, I don't know. *Fond?* Is that the word that comes to mind when I think of Aaron Bravo?"

Jillian made a low, impatient sound. "What I'm getting at is, this is way too sudden, don't you think?

Out of nowhere, you're in love with him? On Valentine's Day?"

Celia nodded. "Yes." Then she shook her head. "No." And then she looked at the ceiling. "Oh, I don't know."

"Well, that clarifies it for me."

"Jilly, I can't be sure if it *started* on Valentine's Day. Maybe…I've loved him for months. Maybe years. But if I did, I didn't know it until a week ago."

Jillian started to say something. But Jane shot her a look. Jillian blew out a breath.

Jane said, "Go on."

Celia poured out her woes. "He doesn't notice me. Not as a whole person. And certainly not as a woman. I'm…a function to him. And it hurts. Bad. Which I know is totally unreasonable. My falling for him wasn't in the job description. He hired a secretary/ assistant. Not a girlfriend. He doesn't *need* a girlfriend. He's got his pick of those."

Jane was nodding grimly. "Showgirls?"

"That's right. *Nice* showgirls, too. I hate that. It makes it even worse, somehow. I can't even despise the competition—not that there *is* any competition."

"Does he seem—" Jillian sought the right words "—as if he *could* be interested, if you told him?"

Slowly, pressing her lips together and swallowing down more tears, Celia shook her head.

"You're *sure* of that?"

Jane jumped in. "Oh, how can she know for sure? She's not objective about this. Look at her. She's gone around the bend over the guy."

"That's right," Jillian said. "Of course, she can't be objective."

"I *can* be objective." Celia protested. "I *am* objective. I'm sure he's not interested in me as a woman."

Jane scooted over and took her by the shoulders. "Look at me, Ceil."

"Fine. Okay." Celia met her friend's eyes.

"Are you sure this is the real thing? Are you sure it's really love? Are you sure it's not—"

"Stop," said Celia. "Yes. I'm sure. It's *all* I'm sure of lately. This is love, I know it. I've known it since V-day. I can't explain it. I can't convince you if you won't believe. But it is the truth. I'm in love with Aaron Bravo."

Jane stared at her for a several long seconds more, her eyes narrowed, probing. Then she whispered, softly, "I see." She let go of Celia's shoulders and went back to her pillows.

Jillian grabbed the bottle and refilled her own glass. "I'm going to ask you again, because I don't think you really gave this question a chance before. Could he *be* interested, if he only knew how you felt?"

"No." Celia sank back against the wall again. "I don't think so. I really don't."

"But you don't *know,* not for certain. You'll never know for certain, not if *he* never knows how you feel."

"I'm certain enough." Celia traced the rim of her glass with her index finger. "I just have to decide whether I can stand this anymore. Or whether I should just…spruce up my résumé and find another place to work.''

Jane and Jillian exchanged looks. Then Jillian said, ''But you love that job. You're making *lots* of money. You have points in the company. And it's only going to get better. Aaron Bravo hasn't gotten where he's going yet. And until now, you've been looking forward to being there when he does.''

''You think I don't know that?''

''And it's only been—what—a week since you realized how you feel about him? You don't need to go rushing into anything too drastic.''

''Jilly, you're not telling me anything I haven't told myself at least a hundred times.''

Jane said, ''Well, here's my opinion. Honesty is the best policy.''

Jillian groaned.

Jane looked vaguely injured. ''All right, so it's a cliché. That doesn't make it any less true.'' She pointed a finger at Celia. ''Tell him how you feel.''

Jillian slapped the edge of coffee table to get their attention. ''No. Hold it. Bad idea.''

''Why?'' demanded Jane. ''Why is telling the truth a bad idea?''

''Because when it comes to love, you should…never ask a question you don't know the answer to.''

Jane winced. ''And *you* get paid to give people advice?''

''Well,'' Celia reminded Jane, ''she mostly gives advice on things like which fork to use and how to get peach-juice stains out of silk blouses.''

''I beg your pardon,'' Jillian huffed. ''I give advice to the lovelorn, if they write in. I'll advise on any subject. That's my job.''

''Scary, very scary,'' muttered Jane.

''I heard that,'' snapped Jillian.

''Sorry.'' Jane adjusted her skirt over her knees.

Jillian said, ''I mean it. There's another way. A *better* way.''

Celia sat forward eagerly. ''All right. *What* way?''

Jillian cleared her throat. ''Absolutely first of all, you have to make him notice you as a woman.''

''Oh,'' said Celia, sinking back, disappointed and letting it show. ''And how do you expect me to do that?''

Jane stopped fiddling with her skirt. ''Oh, my God. I think she's talking makeover.''

It was an old joke between them. Jillian gave her first makeover when the three of them were twelve years old. Jane was her subject. She cut Jane's hair and dyed it—green. Jane wore a hat for months.

Jillian sniffed. ''Oh, come on. In case you've forgotten, I now get paid and paid well to do what you're groaning about. And I act as an *adviser* now—an extremely *knowledgeable* adviser. I let the experts do the actual cutting and coloring. I've come a long way from that first haircut I gave you.''

''And a good thing, too,'' Jane said.

Jillian pulled a face at Jane, then turned to Celia. ''Brighter colors,'' she instructed. ''Softer, more touchable fabrics. We aren't talking beating him over the head with you. We are talking subtle, sexy little changes—and I think you ought to bring out the red in your hair. With that gorgeous pale skin, you'd be a knockout. And you've got those darling rosebud lips—what are those called, those cute, fat old-time dolls with those darling rosebud mouths?''

"Kewpie dolls," Jane supplied. "And you're right—about her lips, anyway. She's got Kewpie-doll lips.''

"Lips that she never makes anything of." Jillian sent Celia an I-mean-business scowl. "A deeper, riper shade of lipstick. Are you with me?''

"She's right," Jane conceded. "You'd look great in brighter colors. Red hair would be good on you—so would darker lipstick. Go there if you want to. But as far as Aaron Bravo goes, *tell him.* Three little words. *I love you.* There is no substitute for honesty. It's the place where every relationship should start. If you let him know how you feel, you give him a chance to—'' The ringing of the telephone cut her off. "Don't you move.''

Celia slumped among her pillows. "Where would I go?''

Jane uncrossed her legs and stood. She went to the phone on the table at the other end of the couch. "Hi, this is Jane… Yes…'' A smug little smile curved her lips. "Of course. Can you hold on? Thanks.'' She punched a button in the headset and turned to Celia, one dark brow lifted.

Celia frowned at her. "For me?''

Now Jane was grinning. "Speak of the devil, as they say.''

Celia's heart started pounding so hard, it felt as though it slammed against the wall of her chest with every beat. It was a very disconcerting sensation. "Aaron?" She more mouthed the word than said it.

Jane nodded.

Jillian let out a short, loud bark of laughter.

"Shh!" Celia reached over and bopped her on the knee. She hissed in whisper, "He'll hear you...."

"No he won't," said Jane. "I've got him on Mute—and did you want to speak with him or not?"

Celia shot to her feet and raced to grab the phone. She put it to her ear. "Hello?"

No one answered.

"Here," said Jane. Celia held out the phone and Jane punched the right button. Celia put it to her ear again, opened her mouth—and shut it. Jane was still standing there, watching expectantly.

Celia made frantic shooing motions. With a sigh, Jane returned to her pillows.

Celia turned away, toward the wide double doors that led to the entrance hall, seeking just a tiny bit of privacy. "Hello. Aaron?"

"Celia. There you are. Good." He sounded preoccupied, as always. Preoccupied and wonderful. His deep, rich voice seemed to pour into her ear and all through her body, melting her midsection, turning her knees to water.

She asked, quite calmly, she thought, "Is something wrong?"

"Wrong? No." She heard the telltale clicking sounds that meant he was sitting at a computer. "I was typing a note to Tony Jarvis...." Anthony Jarvis was Senior Vice-President of Project Development. For Aaron, High Sierra was just one step in the road—a big step, but not the only one. Silver Standard Resorts, High Sierra's parent company, had to keep growing. Tony Jarvis was the main man responsible for scouting future venues. ''The note has vanished. Can't seem to bring it back up.''

She couldn't help grinning. Since he never typed his own e-mails, he'd forgotten the finer points of the program they used for them.

''Celia. Find my memo.''

She told him what to click on.

''Ah,'' he said after a moment. ''There it is. Thank you.''

''No problem—Aaron?''

''Hmm?''

''How did you get this number?''

A pause, then, ''You're irritated, that I called you there?''

''Not at all.'' Never. Ever. Call me anytime. Anywhere. For any reason… ''I just wondered.''

''You said you were going to Jane Elliott's. I called information. It's a listed number.''

He'd remembered that she was going to Jane's! She could hardly believe it. He so rarely remembered anything personal she told him. Her heart pounded even harder, with pure joy. ''Oh. Of course. You called information. I should have known….''

''Celia?'' He sounded puzzled. ''Are you all right?''

''Oh. Yes. Fine. Just fine.''

''Have a good weekend.''

''I will….''

The line went dead. She pulled the phone away

from her ear and stared at it, wild joy fading down to something kind of hollow and dejected.

Really, the call had meant less than nothing to him. She had to face that, had to *accept* it.

Jillian said, "See? He can't live without you."

Celia put down the phone. "That is so not the case." She returned to her spot against the wall, dropped to the floor and flopped back on her pillows.

Jillian was adamant. "He can't live without you. He just doesn't know it yet."

"Tell him," Jane commanded for the third time that night.

"Give *up*," Celia cried. "I'm not telling him. And I'm not changing my hair color, either."

"Then what *will* you do?" asked Jane.

"I haven't decided yet."

Her friends groaned in unison.

They worked on her all weekend, advising, cajoling, prodding and instructing. They wore her down, little by little.

Jane kept pushing honesty. Jillian talked hair and wardrobe and subliminal seduction. Celia moaned and protested and begged them to let it go. They would, for a while—and then they'd start in again.

She couldn't hold firm against them forever. And she loved that they listened to her, that they *cared*. They really were the best friends any woman could have.

By noon Sunday, when she got in her rental car to drive to the Reno airport, she had made a decision.

She would take Jane's advice and tell Aaron of her love.

Chapter Four

Celia's course of action seemed perfectly clear to her when she was waving goodbye on that crisp, snowy Sunday in front of Jane's wonderful old house.

First she would tell Aaron of her feelings. And depending on how he reacted, *maybe* she'd consider some of Jillian's suggestions—if she wasn't too busy nursing a broken heart while pounding the pavement looking for another job.

It was the ''if'' part that ruined her resolve.

Because how could she help fearing that the ''if'' part was reality? She would tell him she loved him. And he would tell *her,* very gently, because he was a kind man at heart, that he was sure she'd be happier working for someone else.

She'd lose him *and* her job.

All right, she was miserable now. But she was miserable and *employed.* She just couldn't see the trade-off. If she told him, she'd still be miserable. And she'd be out of work, as well.

"Oh, that's negative." She'd lie in bed at night, staring up at the dark ceiling, giving herself advice. "I am so negative." She would tell herself, "Celia Louise Tuttle, you've got to snap out this. You've got to give it up, get over him—or tell him how you feel."

Jillian called on Tuesday. "Well? Did you do it? What did he say? How did it go?"

Celia let too long a pause elapse before answering.

Jillian figured it out. "You didn't do it."

"I'm *trying.*"

"Celia. If you're going to do it, do it."

"I will, I will…."

"Tomorrow morning. The minute he comes in the door. Look up from your desk and say, 'I have to speak with you privately about a personal matter.' Get him to set a time. Have him come to your suite."

"Oh, God."

"Better if it's on your turf."

Right, Celia thought. Easier for him to get up and walk out.

"You can do it, Celia."

"Yes. I can. I know…."

The next morning, when he called her in to go over the calendar, she was ready. She truly was. She stood from her desk and she straightened her fawn-colored skirt—brighter colors, hah! Like wearing fire-engine red and Jolly Rancher green could make him love her.

She tucked her yellow legal pad under her arm, grabbed her pencil and her miniature tape recorder and crossed to the high, wide door that led to his private office.

She paused there to smooth her hair and tug on the hem of the jacket that matched the fawn-colored skirt. I'm okay, she thought. Pulled-together. Calm. Collected. Ready to do it.

She pushed open the door and there he was, right where she expected him to be, at his big glass desk in front of the wall of windows, engrossed in something on his computer screen.

She quietly turned and made sure the door was shut. Then she marched across the room and stepped between the two black leather visitors' chairs that faced his desk, planting herself in front of him.

It took him a moment to stop punching keys and look up. His bronze-kissed dark brows drew together. "Celia?"

That was it. All he said. It was way too much. It was, *Is there a problem and do we really need to address it right now?*

No. They didn't.

She sidled to the right, dropped into one of the two chairs, indicated her legal pad and chirped brightly, "Ready when you are."

Jane called next. On Thursday, after midnight. "Did you do it?"

"Oh, Janie."

"You didn't."

"I *almost* did."

"But you didn't."

"It's really...hard for me."

Jane let out a long breath. "Look. I've been thinking...."

Celia clutched the phone as if it were a lifeline. "Yeah?"

"Maybe you're not up for reality right now. Maybe you're not ready to face him with the truth." That was sounding pretty reasonable—until Jane went on. "Maybe you're enjoying this a little, kind of reveling in your misery."

"Jane!" That hurt. It really did. And partly because it had the sharp sting of truth.

She was getting kind of...used to being miserable. Yesterday was two weeks since V-day. Two weeks of suffering. She'd kind of gotten into a groove with it now, hadn't she?

"Celia Louise, you are the classic middle child, you know that you are."

"Is this a lecture coming on?"

"You are a middle child and you know how to be...ignored. Passed over. You don't get out and make things happen like a first child. You don't expect all good to come to you, as the baby in the family always does. You...accept being in the middle. You can easily become stuck."

"And I'm stuck right now, is that what you're saying?"

"Yes. You're stuck in the middle, sitting at the trestle table, clutching your sad little bowl of gruel, knowing when you finish it, you'll still be very, very hungry—and yet unwilling to get up and ask the headmaster for more.''

"My bowl of *gruel?*"

"Come on. You remember. Dickens. *Oliver Twist*. In the orphanage. We read it in Mrs. Oakley's freshman English class."

She remembered. "Shall we go into what happened when Oliver actually got up and asked for more?"

Jane was silent for a count of two. "Okay," she conceded. "Bad analogy."

"No kidding."

"But in the end, Oliver succeeded in *life*. Because he was someone who could get up when he had to and ask for more."

"Hooray for Oliver."

Jane made a small sound in her throat—one that spoke of fading patience. "I'm merely saying, if you don't want to tell him, fine. Maybe you should quit working for him. It wouldn't be the end of the world for you to have to get another job. And at least that would be taking *action*, which I sincerely think it's time for you to do."

There was no getting around it. Jane had it right. "I'll tell him. I will."

"Good. When, exactly?"

"Tomorrow…"

Tomorrow came.

Celia went to the office tower a determined woman.

And when she got there, she learned her boss had taken off for New Jersey on a site-scouting trip with

Tony Jarvis. He wasn't due back until Sunday. He'd left her an e-mail.

TO: Celia Tuttle, clerical/PA
FROM: Aaron Bravo, CEO
SUBJECT: Trip to New Jersey
Back Sunday. Take a three-day weekend. Aaron.

And that meant, unless something came up and he really needed her, she wouldn't see him face-to-face until Monday.

Reprieved, she thought. And felt mingled relief and despair—tinged faintly with worry. As his assistant, it was part of her job to be at his side when he traveled. Why hadn't he wanted her presence on this trip?

She told herself not to make something of nothing. Now and then, he traveled without her. This was probably just one of those times.

She considered going home for another weekend. But she didn't think she could bear facing Jane again until she had done what she'd sworn to do. And there were plenty of projects for her to dig into. She worked all day Friday and half a day on Saturday.

Every time she returned to her rooms, she expected to see the message light blinking on her phone—a call from Jane or Jillian to find out if she'd finally done what she'd vowed to do.

But her friends didn't call. Maybe they'd given up on her. She could hardly blame them if they had.

Sunday, she woke early, thinking, He's due back today....

But she didn't know what time.

And what did it matter what time? She wasn't going to ask him for a private meeting until tomorrow, anyway.

She lasted until noon and then she called his rooms. His machine picked up. Quietly, stealthily—without leaving a message—she returned the phone to its cradle. Then she went to her computer, logged onto the company system, and used her employee code to look up his itinerary. It was unethical, really. Celia Tuttle, secretary/personal assistant didn't need to know exactly when her boss would arrive back in town. But Celia Tuttle, woman hopelessly in love, did.

He was due in at eight that night. Which meant he wouldn't get to his own rooms till nine or ten at the earliest.

It helped to know that. Made it marginally easier not to keep dialing his number and hanging up when his machine answered.

The day dragged by on lead feet. She read the Sunday paper, watched a movie on cable, her mind hardly registering what her eyes were seeing. In the afternoon, she called down to Touch of Gold, High Sierra's full-service luxury spa, and booked the works—mud bath, massage and two-hour facial. Maybe it would help her relax.

It did, while she was down there. And it took up four hours she would have spent stewing. She didn't return to her own rooms until after six.

The rest of the evening was downright unbearable. As eight and nine came and went, she wondered.

Where was he now?

Had he reached the hotel yet?

Was he already in his tower suite—or was he down in the casino somewhere, or in one of High Sierra's luxurious bars or fine restaurants, maybe having a last drink with Tony Jarvis, or possibly courting some recently arrived high rollers?

There was no way to know.

And it didn't even matter. Wherever he was, whatever he was doing, she had no intention of tracking him down tonight, anyway.

She put on her pajamas and she got into bed.

But sleeping fell under the heading, *as if.*

She reached for the phone more than once. But she never picked it up. She knew that if he answered, the sound of his voice would send her into a mindless state of pure panic. She'd hang up without identifying herself—and he would know who it was, anyway. After all, there was such a thing as caller ID.

Which she should have considered earlier, before she'd made that first call.

Jane was so right, she thought, as the night wore on and sleep never came. Here I am, at the bare trestle table, clutching my sad, half-empty bowl of gruel, afraid to stand up and ask for more....

Not sleeping and worrying all night long did nothing for her appearance the next day. She troweled on the concealer to cover the dark pouches beneath her eyes and she put on her nicest suit, which was pale blue, of a particularly fine-gauge gabardine and usually looked very nice on her.

Today, well, nothing she could have worn would have made her look anything better than tired and washed out. Her hair, which was a color somewhere between blond and auburn, seemed flat and lusterless as a brown-paper bag. Her skin looked pasty.

Really, she couldn't help thinking that maybe today just wasn't the day. Maybe she should get to bed early tonight, get a good night's sleep for a change. And then, *tomorrow,* when she felt fresh and didn't look like the walking dead, she could—

"No!" She glared at her own pasty, pale face in the bathroom mirror. "No more excuses. So you look like hell. You're telling him. Today."

She was at her desk when he entered the office suite.

"Good morning, Celia."

Her heart felt as it if had surged straight up into her throat. She swallowed it down and attempted a smile—one that never quite happened.

He was already past her, approaching the door to his private office. "Give me twenty minutes and we'll go over the calendar."

By then, her heart had dropped heavily into her chest again and begun beating so hard and loud she was certain any second she'd go into cardiac arrest. She stood.

"Aaron."

He paused with his hand on the door and turned back to her. He looked puzzled.

Really, now she thought about it, he'd been looking puzzled way too much lately. Probably because she'd been acting so strangely, he couldn't help but notice, even oblivious as he was to her as anything but a function most of the time.

He was waiting—waiting for her to tell him whatever it was she had stopped him to say.

"I...uh..." Her voice sounded awful. Tight. Squeaky.

"Yes?"

She coughed into her hand, to loosen her throat. And then, somehow, she was saying the words she'd been vowing she'd say. "I need to talk with you. Alone. It's a personal matter. I wonder if you would mind stopping by my rooms this evening?" *Suggest a time,* the part of her mind still capable of rational thought instructed frantically. "Uh. About seven?"

He didn't answer for a count of five, at least. He just stood there, looking at her through those blue eyes that really didn't give away much of anything. Finally, he said, rather gently, "Celia. What's this about?"

"I'd rather...wait. To speak with you alone."

He gestured at the outer office, which was decorated in cool grays and midnight blues and was empty except for the two of them. "No one here but you and me. It's as good a time as any to talk. Come on into my office now and we can—"

She put up a hand. "No. Really. I'm sorry, to be so vague about this. But I'd much rather we just kept it to business here in the office. I would honestly appreciate it if you'd just come to my rooms this evening. We'll discuss it there."

He looked at her for a long time. It was absolutely awful. What could he be thinking? Undoubtedly that she was inconveniencing him. Just possibly that he was going to have call down to human resources and get them to find him another PA.

Finally, he said in what seemed a half-hearted attempt at humor, "Well. Am I busy?"

She managed a pained smile. "Uh. No. Not at seven. Not as of now, anyway."

"All right then," he said. "Your rooms. At seven." He turned from her and went through the door to his office, closing it quietly behind him.

Chapter Five

Once in his office, Aaron Bravo stood at the door for a moment, his hand on the doorknob, thinking, *What the hell is up with Celia?*

Then he smelled coffee.

She had it ready for him, as always, waiting on the credenza. He went over, poured himself a cup and drank it right there, staring out the glare-treated glass beyond his desk, not really seeing the city sprawled across the desert landscape below.

He still had Celia on his mind. She didn't look well. Hadn't for a week or two now.

So could she be ill? And if so, was it serious? Was she planning to tell him she needed some time off— or worse, that she'd have to give up her job?

Damn. She was young, too young to be dangerously ill. And he'd sure as hell hate to lose her. She was the next thing to a genius at what she did. Always there when he needed her—and yet never in the way.

Pregnant.

The word popped into his head. He frowned. No. Not Celia. Celia didn't have *time* to get pregnant, not with the kind of demands he made on her. He kept her working hard—too hard, really. He knew that. He also paid her damn well. And he tried to remember to cut her a little slack now and then. Like this last weekend, when he'd let her off the hook for the trip back east, leaving instructions for her to take three days off.

He poured another cup of coffee.

Re the pregnancy angle—on the other hand, why not? How much opportunity did it take, anyway? One encounter could do it. If she hadn't been careful.

Not careful? *Celia?*

Hard to believe. She was such a model of efficiency. He couldn't see her *not* being careful, couldn't imagine her slipping up on something so basic as birth control.

But then, he could hardly imagine Celia *having* sex, let alone dealing with what method of contraception to use. He just didn't think sex when he thought of Celia.

Well, and why the hell should he? She was his *secretary.* And her sex life was her business.

However, accidents did happen. And if she now had a baby on the way...

Well, if she did, okay. It should be manageable.

He'd be willing to deal with a kid in the picture.

They could work around it, if she wanted to stay with him. It might be tough. There'd be some serious inconveniences for both of them. But his mother had done it; raising three sons and running the Highgrade all on her own after his father, the notorious Blake Bravo, had supposedly died.

Yeah. They could work it out if she was going to be a single mom.

But what if there was a man in the picture, too? What if, as busy as he kept her, she'd somehow managed to find herself a guy, a nice stable nine-to-five type who'd want her home every night when he got off work?

Strange. The idea of some stable, ordinary guy stealing Celia away rankled more than a little. He scowled.

The woman would not be easy to replace. Aaron's work was demanding and often chaotic. Celia made sure the chaos was kept to a minimum, and she did it so well that most of the time he was able to take her completely for granted—or he had been, until the last couple of weeks.

And damn it, he wanted things back as they had been. He wanted her problem—whatever it was—solved, so that he could go back to enjoying the benefits of taking her for granted.

He carried his half-full coffee cup to his desk.

Maybe it was something to do with her parents....

He turned on his computer and sat back as it booted.

Hadn't she said that they'd retired and lived in

Phoenix now? How old were they, anyway? Maybe they were failing and needed more of her time.

Time...

He glanced at his Rolex. Ten minutes had passed since he'd entered his office.

And he'd spent most of it staring into space, worrying about his assistant.

It was counterproductive in the extreme. An assistant was supposed to decrease the worry quotient, not herself be a source of concern.

He wasn't going to know for certain what was bothering her until that night. Why stew about it now when there really wasn't a damn thing he could do?

Good question—and one to which he had no answer.

As a rule, Aaron Bravo was not a man who borrowed trouble. He effectively compartmentalized his thinking, gathering facts first and foremost, avoiding what-ifs, never getting hung up on things he could do nothing about. After what he supposed could be called a troubled and turbulent early youth—no way of escaping turbulence with Caitlin Bravo for a mother—he'd realized at the age of seventeen that he wanted money and he wanted to run things. Big time. Neither was going to happen unless he changed his ways.

He had.

And look at him now.

He hadn't gotten where he was by wasting mental energy.

Therefore, he would forget the problem of Celia for now. No sense in trying to come up with answers when he didn't even know what the questions were. She'd tell him what was up tonight and then he could decide what to do about it.

His copy of the *Wall Street Journal* was waiting at his elbow. He picked it up. While he read, he paused now and then to check his various stocks online.

Ten minutes later, Celia tapped on his door armed with that little tape recorder of hers and her trusty notepad. They went over the calendar for the day. She didn't mention her mysterious problem again, kept things strictly on business, which was great with him.

He left the office at ten for a meeting with his vice-presidents.

After the meeting, he met Jennifer for lunch at one.

Jennifer was charming and funny, as always. And so easy on the eyes. She wore the ruby heart he'd given her for Valentine's Day.

She touched it, lightly, and beamed her beautiful smile at him. "Aaron, I love it. You always know just what to get for a woman…"

He looked at the heart, riding just above Jennifer's spectacular left breast and a vague irritation moved through him, a…dissatisfaction, a sense of unease.

Celia. Her name came into his mind in spite of the fact that he'd decided not to have it there.

Celia had picked out that heart. She had an unerring sense of what to choose when he asked her to go out and find a gift.

If Celia quit, he'd have to find another assistant. A stranger. Someone…not from home. Some other woman—or man—would compose his e-mails, tell him where to look for files he couldn't find, buy trinkets for his girlfriends....

"Aaron? What is it, *caro?*"

"Hm?"

"You are thousands of miles away." She stuck out her full lower lip in a playful pout.

"I'm right here." He reached across the table and took her hand. "And I'm glad you like the pin."

"I do." She squeezed his hand. She must have slid off her shoe, because under the table, she was lifting his pants leg with her bare toe. "Allow me to prove my gratitude...."

That afternoon, he met with his managers. Celia was there, at his right hand, as always. After the meeting, they both returned to the office. He closeted himself with Tony Jarvis for a couple of hours. They discussed the failing casino they'd looked at in Atlantic City. A grind joint, as they said in the gaming business. A grind joint catered to low rollers, everyday Joes who bet small. Aaron had got his start in Vegas in a grind joint downtown in Glitter Gulch, right on Fremont Street not far from the big neon cowboy known as Vegas Vic. There was good money to be made catering to the grind trade, though buying and sprucing up small casinos was not the focus of Silver Standard Resorts. Still, Tony thought they should take the place, give it a general face-lift and rake in the profits. His numbers were solid. Aaron agreed they would bring it before the board.

It was six-forty when Tony left. Celia was long gone by then. Unless he needed her to stay late for

something, she always left the office tower at around
five-thirty—with the understanding that he could
reach her just about any time should the necessity
arise.

He often had her with him at dinner, when he en-
tertained high rollers or board members or potential
investors. Celia was attractive, but, unlike Jennifer
and the other breathtaking women he had dated, she
was not the kind of attractive that distracted anyone
from the business at hand. And it often came in handy
to have his secretary right there beside him. She remembered what was on his calendar. She would immediately take steps to solve any minor problem that
came up. And sometimes, she picked up on things he
didn't—what his people were up to, what they might
be dissatisfied over. Or what minor insurrections
might be brewing among his managers.

But she wouldn't be sitting beside him at dinner
tonight.

No, tonight he would be meeting her alone.

In her rooms.

Celia stood in her bedroom, wearing only a sky-
blue bra and matching panties. Most of the contents
of her walk-in closet lay strewn across the queen-
sized bed. She'd been trying on clothes and discard-
ing them in disgust for over an hour now. She'd
planned to decide what to wear, take a soothing half-
hour bath, then put on fresh makeup and fix her hair.

So much for that soothing bath. Too bad about the
makeup and the hair.

It was 6:57. Aaron would be at her door some time

in the next four or five minutes, and she hadn't even gotten past choosing what to wear.

Nothing looked right. She tugged an eggplant-colored ankle-length knit skirt from the pile and shook it out, thinking, well, at least it's not gray.

She had discovered, in her extended search through her closet the past hour, that she owned way too many outfits in varying shades of gray.

Brighter colors, Jillian had advised. Celia hated to admit it, but she was beginning to think that Jilly was right—and she fervently wished she had seen the light sooner.

Now, it was too late. No time for a last-minute shopping spree. She *had* to make a choice from the mostly gray pile in front of her.

She stepped into the skirt, settled the elastic waist-band in place, smoothed it with both hands and then dug the matching boat-neck tunic top out of the tangle on the bed. She shook it out and glared at it. It, like the skirt, was one of those packable knits, the kind that never wrinkled. There was nothing *wrong* with it. In fact, like the skirt, it had something major going for it, in that it was not gray.

Too bad it was just so…not what she had in mind. Everything in her closet was utterly and completely *not* what she had in mind. Not for this. Not for the moment when she told her boss that somehow she'd managed to fall madly and hopelessly in love with him.

She groaned at the tunic.

And right then she heard the buzzer that meant there was someone at her door.

Celia muttered a very bad swear word. She tossed the tunic back on the bed and wriggled out of the skirt.

Now what? She had to choose something. And she had to choose fast.

A swatch of lustrous silk caught her eye—okay, it was gray. But the fabric was beautiful, nubby with a gorgeous sheen. She grabbed for it—a pair of pants, flat front, tapered legs. That, and her nicest white silk blouse.

Best she could do, given what was available.

She yanked on the pants and grabbed for the blouse, sticking her arms in the sleeves, tugging it onto her shoulders. Zipping and buttoning, she raced for the closet, where she stuck her feet in a pair of plain black-suede ballet flats.

The buzzer sounded again. "Coming, coming," she whispered under her breath as she paused to look at herself in the full-length closet mirror.

It was…okay. Not great. But okay.

She smoothed her not-quite blond and not-quite auburn hair and tugged on the hem of the blouse. She needed lipstick, at least.

But there was no time.

With a tiny, frustrated cry, she turned and rushed from the room, pausing only to pull the door shut behind her so that, if for some unknown reason he ended up in her hallway, he would not be able to see the disaster she'd made of her bed.

The buzzer sounded for the third time just as she got to the front door.

"Sorry," she said breathlessly, when she pulled it

back and found him standing there, frowning. "I was just—" She cut herself off. Jeez. Like he needed to know what she'd put herself through in order to end up in a white blouse, gray pants and a pair of flat-heeled black shoes. She waved a hand—airily, she hoped. "Well. Come on in." She stepped back and he stepped forward. She closed the door behind him.

"Can I take your jacket?" He was still wearing the gorgeous gray silk suit he'd been wearing earlier, when he disappeared into his office with Anthony Jarvis—and why was it, she wanted to know, that he had to look so splendid in gray? *She* ought to look that good in gray. She certainly had enough of it.

"Great." He slid the jacket off and handed it to her. She hung it in the small closet next to her front door, breathing a tiny sigh of relief once she got it on the hanger and in the closet. She wasn't visibly shaking, thank God. But inside, every atom seemed to be quivering. It would have been all too easy to fumble and drop it.

"This way." She led him out of her small entrance hall and into the living room of her suite—which was a full apartment, complete with kitchen, loft office above the living area, and a bath for each of the two bedrooms.

He looked around him, at her wine-red sofa and buff-colored easy chairs strewn with a number of big pillows in bold prints.

At first, her apartment had been pretty much hotel-issue. It was furnished when she moved in and she lived in it as it was—no hardship, as accommodations at High Sierra were of the best quality. But over time, she'd made her own choices and substituted things she found herself for what the resort had originally provided. Just last year she'd done the living area walls over in sponge-mottled mustard and olive. And she'd bought an old low plank-topped table, had it refinished, and now used it for a coffee table. Her rooms, she realized at that moment, had a lot more variety and visual interest than her wardrobe.

"Nice," he said.

Her smitten heart soared at that monosyllable of a compliment. "Thank you. Uh. Drink?"

"I'll pass." He stood a few feet from one of the easy chairs, waiting for her to tell him why she'd insisted he come here.

"Okay. Well. Have a seat, why don't you?"

He moved in front of the chair and sat down. She perched across from him, on the edge of the red sofa, behind her attractively refinished plank coffee table.

"Well," she said, and smoothed the knees of the gray silk pants it had taken her over an hour to choose. "Okay…"

He waited.

She found she was gnawing the inside of her lip and made herself stop. "I…" she began. But that was all that would come out.

Her whole body felt numb. Numb and too hot and yet shivery at the same time. There was a ringing in her ears, her heart was beating so hard.

She could not do this.

She did not know how to do this.

Aaron leaned forward, his brow furrowed, that

wonderful angular face a portrait of honest concern. "Celia. Please."

She tried again. And the same thing happened. She managed, "I…" and that was all.

"Look," he said carefully. "Whatever's bothering you, whatever's…come up in your life, I'm sure we can work through it. That we can find a way to deal with it. We've been together for long enough now. You should know that you can trust me, can…come to me, if there's a problem."

"I…well, I…"

"You do know that, don't you? That you can come to me?"

"I…yes, well, um…" She swallowed.

"Damn it, Celia." He stood, stuck his hands in his pockets, turned and paced the width of the room, then spun on his heel and paced back again. He stopped in front of her. "What the hell is the matter? Are you sick, is that it? Or…well, just tell me. Are you pregnant?"

She stared up at him, stunned. "Uh. Pregnant?"

"Well. Are you? And I'll tell you right now, if you are, it's okay with me. If you want to keep your job with me, you've got it. I'm not going to get rid of you just because there's a baby on the way. If you think you can handle a child and your job, I'll take your word for it. Because I know your word is good."

"Aaron."

"If that's what you want, I mean. You know what your job entails, the kind of demands that I put on you. You know what you can handle, don't you?"

"Aaron."

"Don't you?"

"Yes, but—"

"But what?"

"Aaron, I'm not."

"Not?"

"Right. Not—"

"Sick?"

"Right."

"Pregnant?"

"Yes…I mean, no. I'm not pregnant, either."

"Well." He stepped back. "All right." He looked at her sideways. "Your parents, then? Is that it?"

"It?"

"Are your parents the problem?"

"No."

"Not your parents…"

"No, they're fine. Retired. Taking it easy."

"In Phoenix."

Her heart lifted. "You remembered."

"What I mean is, they're getting older, right? You have to start spending more time with them. They need to feel they can count on you…."

"No. I told you. They're fine. Both healthy. So far…"

"Fine? Healthy?"

"Yes."

He threw up both hands. "Then, Celia, what?"

"Aaron…"

"Yeah?"

"Aaron, I…"

"Damn it, *what?*"

"Aaron, I love you. I'm sorry, I can't help myself. I love you. I do."

Chapter Six

Aaron backed up until he reached his chair again. Very carefully, he lowered himself into it.

Right then, he stiffened. Celia recognized the expression. He had his cell phone on Silent Page and it had just vibrated.

"It's all right," she said. "Go ahead and answer it."

He pulled the phone from his pocket, glanced at the display, then answered, "What?" He listened, nodded. "Okay… No… Great. Do it now…." He spoke into the phone, but those blue eyes were focused on her.

What she saw in those eyes wasn't good. Her declaration had come as a very big surprise. And not a welcome one.

"All right," he said to whoever was on the other end of the line. "Fine." Then he flipped the phone shut and stuck it back in the pocket of his shirt. He shook his head. "Sorry."

"No problem," she said, because it wasn't—not the phone call anyway.

The rest of it, her asking him to come here to her private rooms, her confession of love, the look on his face right then—well, for all that, *problem* was way too small a word.

And what now?

She stared at him and he stared at her and neither of them seemed to know what to do or say next.

Correction.

She did know one thing.

She knew she would go around the bend if she continued just sitting there. She shot from the couch like a sprung rubber band—then hovered at the edge of the coffee table, stuck on the verge of taking a step.

"Oh, God," she whispered miserably. She looked down at herself, wondered what she was doing standing up. She wasn't going anywhere. She sank to the cushions again.

Aaron said, oh-so-cautiously, "Celia. What can I tell you? I...didn't have a clue."

She could barely contain her own nervous energy, had to fold her hands tightly to keep them from fiddling with the hem of her boring white shirt. "Yes. I can see that."

"I honestly don't know what to say."

"Right. That's pretty obvious, too."

Another bleak and yawning silence followed.

She was the one who broke it, her voice, out of nowhere surprisingly calm. "You know, I've never seen you look terrified before."

He made a low sound in his throat. "That's ridiculous. I'm not terrified."

A small, dry laugh escaped her. "Oh, yes you are."

"No." He shifted in the chair. "No, that's not true."

She opened her mouth to argue some more, then shut it without letting anything get out. He looked pretty scared to her, but if he didn't want to admit it, that was certainly his right.

And maybe she was reading him all wrong, anyway. After all, he'd yet to actually *say* he wasn't interested.

"Aaron. Please. I just want to know if, well, I mean, if there's any possibility that you might—"

He put up a hand, a warding-off kind of gesture. "Celia," he said. It was enough, just her name. The way he said it, so carefully, so…uncomfortably, told her everything she needed to know, though he still had yet to actually put it in words. "I'm flattered, I am. But I'm not what someone like you should be looking for."

"Someone like me?"

"Yes. Someone like you. And that's a compliment."

"A compliment."

"Yes. You are stable and smart, with both feet on the ground. Someone like you deserves the very best in a man."

Oh, why wouldn't he just say it? "Aaron."

"What?"

"In other words, you're not interested."

"Celia—"

"Just say it. Please. Just say it right now."

"Celia…"

"No, listen."

"All right. What?"

"You are not doing me any favor by not saying it."

He let out a long breath. "Okay. I'm not interested."

She'd thought things had gotten as bad as they could get. But somehow, hearing him say it out loud managed to make it all even worse.

And why was she just sitting there? She couldn't bear that, to just sit there.

She shot to a standing position again—which didn't help anything. Oh, she was the biggest fool in all of Las Vegas. And that was saying something, because Las Vegas, everyone knew, was chock full of fools who gambled everything they had—and ended up busted.

As Celia Tuttle was right now.

She started to sit—again—and then stopped herself. It was too ridiculous, to keep popping up and down like that. She was not going to do that anymore. She remained standing, head high, shoulders back.

She really could not fault him, she realized through her own misery, for the way he was handling this. She could see the concern in his eyes, mingled with something else…what was it?

Ah, yes. Embarrassment.

He hated being put in this position, he'd rather be anywhere but here. Still, he hadn't gotten up and walked out. He didn't want to hurt her any more than she was already hurting.

To her tender heart, that was just one more proof of his basic loveableness—that he could be so very, very *sweet* about this, in of spite how agonizingly awful it all was.

"Aaron, I am so sorry." She took a step toward him, but he stiffened, a tiny movement that nonetheless spoke of pure dread. She put out both hands in a placating gesture. "Don't worry. I won't...come near you." He opened his mouth to say something, but she couldn't let him. Not until she'd made some kind of attempt to explain herself. "Oh, I do hate that I did this, that I put you on the spot like this. I just...well, I didn't know what else to do. I've been so miserable, since I realized that I..." She didn't finish. How could she, with him staring at her as though the only thing he wanted was out of that room?

She closed her eyes, sucked in a breath and let it out in a rush. "Oh, why am I telling you this?" She hung her head. "You poor man. You obviously don't need to hear it."

"Celia." His concern for her must have overcome his dread that she might physically throw herself on him. He rose again and took a step toward her. "It's okay. Honestly."

How could he say that? "No." She looked up and glared at him. "It is not, in any way, okay."

He froze where he was.

She felt about an inch high. "Oh, look at me. This is terrible. Now I'm snapping at you. Please. Forgive me."

"Of course."

She managed a grim smile. "I may be acting like an insane person. But I promise, I honestly do realize that this is not your fault."

"Well," he said gently. "That's something."

She didn't know what to say next.

Apparently, neither did he.

The silence stretched out, a great, gaping hole of it. They stared at each other, both of them just standing there, about four feet apart in the middle of her living room.

At last, she said, "All right. I'll tell you what. Tomorrow morning, you'll have my formal resignation."

He frowned. "Why?"

She was certain she hadn't heard him right. "Huh?"

"I said, why? Do you want to quit working for me?"

"Well. That's hardly the question."

"Sure it is. Do you?"

"Well, come on. I mean, this changes everything, don't you think?"

"Not necessarily."

What was it about men? They could be so thick-headed sometimes. "Aaron. Come on. Do you honestly think it's going to be possible for us to go on working together now, after this?"

"It's certainly possible for me." He looked at her levelly. "How about you? Do you *want* to turn in your resignation now, is that it?"

"Well, wouldn't that be for the best?"

"From my point of view, no, not at all. I'd rather you didn't."

"You would?"

"That's right. We have a hell of a fine working relationship. I don't want to lose that if I don't have to. You can always hand in a letter of resignation later. But give it a while, why don't you? See how you feel, now your big secret is out?"

How she felt, right that moment, was vaguely insulted. "'My big secret'? You make it sound like a joke."

"Celia. Honestly. That's not my intention. I'm just saying, give it a chance. Maybe it won't work. Maybe you'll be unhappy and I'll be uncomfortable and we'll both end up admitting we'd be better off if you went elsewhere. But for right now, you like your job, right?" She didn't answer immediately, so he prodded, "Well, do you?"

"Yes. I do. Very much."

"Good. You like your job and I like the way you do your job. Why turn our backs on that unless we absolutely have to?"

Was he right? Could it work? "You're saying we'll more or less pretend this conversation never happened? We'll try to go on as we were before?"

"Exactly."

"Do you really believe that's possible?"

"I wouldn't suggest it if I didn't."

She tipped her head to the side and studied him through narrowed eyes. "I just don't know...."

"Sure you do. You give it a try. If after a few weeks, you find you're unhappy, you give your notice. Simple as that."

Chapter Seven

Five minutes later, Aaron stood in the hall outside Celia's rooms shaking his head.

She thought she was in love with him.

He couldn't believe it. Smart, cool-headed Celia Tuttle had more sense than that. He was sure she'd get over it—and soon, he hoped. Pulling his phone from his pocket, he headed for the elevators.

By the time he reached the ground floor, he'd made two calls, one to Tony Jarvis concerning a small point that had been nagging him about that New Jersey casino, the other to the manager who had called him while he was in Celia's rooms. Tony answered Aaron's question, and the manager reported that his problem had been solved.

The mirrored elevator doors parted. Aaron stuck

the phone back in his pocket and stepped out into the greedy heart of High Sierra, her 110,000-square-foot casino.

Aaron liked to walk the floor. He found it soothing. He liked the sounds he heard there—the electronic ringing of slot machines, the clink of coins cascading into chrome trays, even the occasional triumphant cry of some lucky sucker who had managed, for once, to buck the odds and beat the house. He liked to see things running smoothly. And he knew that the dealers and pit bosses, the stickmen and floor managers, the cocktail waitresses and change girls all worked a little harder and played things just a little straighter because the chairman of the board and CEO of Silver Standard Resorts lived on-site. They knew that there was no telling when he might decide to come down from his tower office or his penthouse suite and wander among them—and they modified their behavior accordingly.

Silver Standard had a reputation as a company that promoted for talent and performance, that *juice*—the old Wise-Guy word for influence—didn't mean near as much when you worked at High Sierra as it did at a lot of the other casino/hotels along the strip. It was still Las Vegas and who you knew mattered. But in Aaron's book, *what* you knew and how good you were at what you did counted, too.

He'd grown up around gaming. There was always a card game going on in the back room of the Highgrade. His mother ran her own small-time version of keno, and slots lined the walls. Aaron and his brothers had never had much of what most people thought of as a family life. But all three of them could spot a con a mile away. And they knew most of the thousands of ways to cheat.

That night, Aaron stood near one of the roulette tables and watched a couple of idiots try one of the oldest scams in the book. The first guy—the decoy— placed a late bet, distracting the dealer, so his buddy could lay down his cash *after* the roulette ball had fallen onto the winning number. The cheat was so common, it even had a name: past-posting—and the cash itself was another dead giveaway, since most gamblers bet with casino checks.

The dealer had blown it, allowing herself to be taken in by the decoy, giving him her attention as she explained that it was too late for him to bet. But the eye in the sky—the security cameras located all over the casino—recorded everything. And the "mucker," who helped the dealer clear the table of losing bets, was on the job. He saw the second man past-post his bet. The pit boss appeared with a couple of security guards. The two would-be scam artists were escorted from the table with a minimum of fuss.

Aaron moved on, spent some time watching the blackjack tables, and then observing the action at craps, which everyone knew was the true gamblers' game, fast and exciting, not for the shy or faint of heart.

He spotted his cousin, Jonas Bravo, the famous Bravo Billionaire, rolling dice, his sexy blond wife, Emma, at his side. The Bravo Billionaire gambled for relaxation. He kept five hundred thousand on deposit in High Sierra's cage. And Aaron knew for a fact that he kept similar deposits at most of the other major resort/casinos on the strip.

Aaron knew a lot about his wealthy, powerful cousin. And he had no doubt that his cousin knew about him. But they never spoke. Aaron's father, after all, had been Blake Bravo, the blacker-than-black sheep of the Los Angeles Bravos, a man who had done murder and worse. The connection between the two branches of the family had been severed before either Aaron or Jonas was born.

Aaron watched, keeping well back, as the cousin he'd never met placed bets and won more than he lost. His pretty wife laughed and clapped her hands every time Jonas added to the stacks of checks in front of him, occasionally blowing an errant platinum curl out of her shining eyes.

Aaron should have moved on long before he did. But he found the sight intriguing. His cousin and his cousin's wife. Married for—what? About six months now, according to the scandal sheets. And happy together. Now and then, they'd glance at each other. Heat would arc. And more than heat. Affection, too. Yeah. A blind man could see there was a real bond between the Bravo Billionaire and his blond bombshell of a wife.

Celia came to mind—which was logical, given what had transpired in her rooms less than an hour ago. Clearly Celia wanted a Jonas-and-Emma-Bravo kind of bond in her life. She was a good woman, one who certainly deserved to get what she wanted. He probably should have let her quit, let her find another job—and another man to pin her hopes on. Too bad a good secretary was so damned hard to find.

Also too bad that the Bravo Billionaire's wife had spotted him. He'd spaced off for a second or two there, on the subject of Celia. And now Emma Bravo was staring right at him, those shining eyes wide, her lush mouth a round *O*. She grabbed her husband by the arm and whispered something in his ear.

Aaron faded backward, turning and striding off, disappearing into the crowd, eliminating the possibility that he and his long-lost cousin might actually make eye contact. Aaron didn't need contact of any kind with Jonas, or any other estranged Bravo relatives. He had enough trouble with the Bravos he already knew—his two brothers and his wild-hearted, short-tempered, heavy-handed mother.

The phone in his pocket started vibrating as he entered the Forty-Niner, the smallest of High Sierra's six bars. He sat down at the end of the bar, signaling the bartender for his usual. Then he pulled the phone out and answered it without pausing to check the caller ID display.

Big mistake.

"Hello, my darlin' boy." Speak of the devil, as they say. "How come you never call your poor old mother?" Caitlin Bravo had a voice like no other. Rough and low, a voice that spoke of smoky rooms and strong whiskey and the risky temptations of bold games of chance.

"Did I give you this number?"

"Aaron. Don't get smart with me."

"What do you want, Ma?"

"I told you. A phone call. A visit. I miss your bad attitude and your sweet, handsome face."

The bartender set his drink in front of him. Aaron laid down a generous tip. "Is there some kind of problem?"

"Yeah. I never see my boys. Cade hasn't been around for a couple of weeks now. He's supposed to be moving back to town—did you hear?"

Aaron sipped his whiskey. "He bought that place next to the old Elliott house, right?"

"That's right. He's been fixin' it up, or so I've heard. But I haven't seen him. And you know Will. Off in Sacramento all the time, doing whatever lawyers do in their fancy suits. And then there's you, Mr. Las Vegas, Mr. Chairman of the Board. Damn it, I miss you. I truly do."

Aaron had a pretty good idea of what had inspired this excess of motherly feeling. He'd bet and bet large that Caitlin's latest boyfriend, a Nordic type, younger than Aaron, with muscles on his muscles and shoulder-length blond hair, had moved on. "What happened to Hans?"

"Nothing lasts forever, my darlin', and you know it, too. Come home. I'll wish you a happy birthday in person." She'd remembered. His birthday was that Friday. "I'll bake you a cake."

"When did you ever bake a cake?"

"So I've been known to exaggerate." He could hear the shrug in her voice. "There's a new bakery around the corner. I'll give them a call. Have them send one over, with your name on it and thirty-five birthday candles." Her tone turned wheedling.

"Come on. Come home. Blow out your candles, do my taxes...."

Aaron said nothing. He didn't like what he'd just heard.

"Yoo-hoo, you still there, birthday boy?"

"Ma. What happened to the accountant I found for you?"

"A stranger from California—and Modesto, at that? You know very well that I couldn't trust him."

"He was a damn good man."

"Look. When it comes to my money, I don't want a hired gun. I want my own flesh and blood on it, you know that."

"Caitlin, I have a corporation to run. I don't have time anymore to personally fill out your Schedule C."

"Come home. This weekend. It's two days. You can spare it."

"I'll see what I can do."

"I know what that means. Something will come up, you just haven't decided what yet."

So okay, she did know him better than he often gave her credit for. "Maybe. In a week or two."

"No maybes. You come here this weekend, or I come there."

That did it. Every time she showed up at High Sierra, she drove him absolutely nuts. She couldn't just yank the one-armed bandit and get in a little shopping the way any normal fifty-four-year old woman on a visit to Vegas would do. She had to walk the floor, hang over the shoulders of his dealers and his boxmen, barge into his office every few hours with endless criticisms of the way things were run and detailed advice as to how he could make it all better.

"Aaron? You still there?"

"I'm here."

"Well?"

He could hear it in that whiskey voice of hers. She knew she had him.

"All right, all right. I'll fly up Friday night. And you said it—only for a day or two."

"Thank you, my darlin'," she replied, oh-so-sweetly. "See you then."

Aaron put his phone in his pocket, finished his drink and signaled for one more. He was halfway through that second whiskey when he decided he'd ask Celia to go with him on Friday. After all, New Venice was her hometown, too. She could see her friend, Jane.

Also, Celia *was* a CPA. When Caitlin started in on him again about doing her taxes, he could put Celia on it. He could point out that he trusted Celia implicitly—which he did—and that she was, after all, a hometown girl. Not Caitlin's flesh and blood, admittedly, but almost as good.

Yeah, okay. His mother wasn't all that easy to deal with. She'd probably drive Celia as nuts as she drove him. Celia would find herself wondering how she ever could have thought herself in love with someone who had a mother like that.

And what was wrong with that?

Not a damn thing.

Celia needed to get over him and if his overbearing, loudmouthed mother helped her do that, well, great.

Everybody wins.

He brought up the weekend the next morning, when she came in his office to go over the calendar.

"Celia, about this weekend…"

"What about it?" Her tone was pleasant and professional. He watched her settle into one of the chairs opposite his desk and fiddle with her little tape recorder.

She definitely looked better. More relaxed. Not so stressed out as she had in the past couple of weeks. The dark circles he'd noticed under her eyes last night had faded to faint smudges this morning. Her pale cheeks looked pinker. There was a bloom on her skin.

Apparently, he thought wryly, getting her grand passion for him off her chest had been good for her. "You know, you look great today."

"Thank you."

Aaron was right.

Celia *was* feeling better.

She'd laid her deep secret on him. He'd turned her down. It had hurt. She'd been terribly embarrassed.

But the world hadn't ended.

Yes, she still loved him. However, he didn't love her and he'd told her straight out that there was no chance he ever would. She could accept that. Now, she'd decided over the light meal of broiled chicken and Caesar salad she'd fixed for herself after he'd left her rooms, she could start getting over him.

She'd cleared off her bed and hung her clothes back in her closet and turned in around ten. And for the first time in several days, she had slept through the night.

Celia set the tape recorder on the edge of the wide glass desk, then sat back in her chair, resting her elbows on the arms and folding her hands lightly over the legal pad that waited in her lap. She gave her boss a bright, attentive smile to show him she was listening to whatever it was he had to say to her. "Okay, now. About the weekend?"

"Ah," he said. "Yes. I have to fly home Friday. I'll return Sunday. I'd like you to come with me, if that will work for you."

An absurd little thrill shivered through her. He wanted her with him for the weekend! Now, wasn't that wonderful?

But almost as fast as it went zinging through her, the thrill faded.

She reminded herself of what he'd said last night. He wasn't interested in her romantically—and there was no chance he would *get* interested.

So why, all of a sudden, did he want to take her home with him?

"Is Silver Standard scouting properties in New Venice now?"

"Scouting properties?" he repeated, sounding way too vague for her peace of mind. "No. This will be a personal visit."

She pondered that information. "A personal visit…"

He leaned back in his chair and regarded her through hooded eyes. "Is there a problem? I thought you'd be pleased at the idea of a trip home."

She almost smiled. Men. You told them you loved them and they suddenly thought you had *sucker* scrawled across your forehead. "Your mother called, right?"

That deep blue gaze slid away. All of a sudden, something really interesting was happening on his computer screen.

She waited while he typed a series of commands and did the point-and-click shuffle with the mouse. And then he decided he had a call to make, one that just couldn't wait.

"Give me a moment?"

"Of course."

He picked up the phone on his desk and punched up a number from auto-dial. When the other party answered, he fired off a series of quick questions and brief commands. "Fine," he said in conclusion. "All right. See to it." He dropped the receiver back into its cradle and resumed pointing and clicking with the computer mouse. "Hm," he said. "Ah." Finally, he faced her. "Celia."

She lifted an eyebrow to show him that he had her full attention.

He grunted. "There's no doubt about it."

"Yes?"

"You know too much."

She grinned. "I do, don't I? What did she want?"

"To see me."

"Any special reason?"

"My birthday's coming."

She already knew that, of course. She'd bought him a silver money clip engraved with his initials back in

January when she'd made the rounds of the after-holiday sales. Since she'd started working for him, she'd always bought him small, thoughtful gifts for birthdays and at Christmas—a pair of cufflinks, a tie that matched his eyes. She knew he liked the things she chose because he wore them—or used them, as the case might be. In return, he gave her bonuses on her birthday and at Christmas. Big ones, which she very much appreciated.

He added, grudgingly, "She's ordering a cake, evidently. With thirty-five candles and Happy Birthday, Aaron, in fancy lettering across the top."

Celia tipped her head to the side. "Hm," she said, nodding, giving him her most patient smile.

"Damn it. All right. Tax time's coming up again."

Ah, thought Celia, we approach the truth at last. "How could I have forgotten?" Every year, getting Caitlin's taxes done was a problem. She wanted them done by someone she trusted. She trusted three people: Aaron, Will and Cade Bravo. Since Aaron was the one with the degree in finance, she inevitably hounded him to do the honors. "But I thought you finally found someone for her."

"Apparently, she fired him."

"So she's after you again?"

"Right."

"But what has that got to do with…" In mid-sentence, the light dawned. "Oh. Aaron," she groaned. "No."

"Help me out here, Celia. Please?"

She should have refused. Right then. Her job description had a lot of leeway in it, but even a personal assistant who had to be ready for just about anything couldn't be expected to do her boss's mother's taxes.

But her "no" got stuck in her throat. He just looked so pitiful. "Listen," she said, reasoning with him when she knew that she ought to be holding her ground with an unequivocal no. "If she wasn't satisfied with the CPA you hired last year, she's not going to be satisfied with me."

"She might. You *are* an accountant."

"I was. But I hated it. That's why I'm not an accountant anymore."

"But you can do the work."

"I was in audit, you know that. Never the tax department."

"You're as qualified to do it as I am—hell. More so."

"No, I'm not. Let's face facts here. Only *you* are qualified because *you* are her son."

"Will you just come with me? Let's just give it a try."

The problem was, when he looked at her like that, so hopefully, so…vulnerable, it was way too easy to forget how she intended to get over him. Way too easy to imagine what a trip home with him might be like, hanging with him at the Highgrade, getting to know his crazy mother, who, whatever anyone said about her, was always very entertaining.

And worst of all, when he looked at her like that, she couldn't help but start imagining that there might be hope for the two of them, in spite of what he'd said last night. That maybe, subconsciously, he was interested in her, after all.

And he knew it, damn him. He was using her own heart against her, the rat.

She spoke in a pleasant tone, but she said what she was thinking. "This is really low of you, Aaron, you know that?"

He met her eyes straight on then, didn't hide behind his computer or his telephone. And he had the grace to look faintly—and also oh-so-attractively—ashamed of himself. "What can I say? I'm a desperate man."

"I should refuse to do this."

He gave her a thoroughly heart-stopping hopeful grin. "Was that a yes I just heard?"

She glared at him.

"Please, Celia. Just give this a try. If anyone can handle my mother, I have a feeling you're the one."

"Wonderful. And if I *can't* handle her?"

"If it doesn't work out and you find she drives you as insane as she makes me, just say so. Believe me, I'll understand."

"You'll pull me off it if I say I want off?"

He winced. "I'm hoping that won't happen, but if it does, just speak up and you're off it. You have my word."

The problem was, she'd started thinking, *Why not?* She had no desire to go back to accounting work full-time, but she did have the skills and she might as well use them.

And, okay, she had to admit, it was lovely to have him look at her so *hopefully.* If she said yes, he'd be grateful.

Now, *that* would be pleasing....

He was waiting for an answer. She said, "I shouldn't…"

"That *is* a yes. Admit it."

"There are conditions."

"Name them."

"I'll prepare your mother's taxes. But I won't take payment—and don't give me that look. If I take payment, I have to sign as the preparer and that makes me liable. I don't want that, Aaron."

He nodded. "Yes. Of course. I understand."

"You'll have to go over my work and approve it, so maybe you'd be better off to just find another CPA with a tax background to do the job—or give in and do it yourself."

"No—to both suggestions. Just give my way a try. You deal with her, getting everything together. Frankly, that's where the real headaches come in for me. Then you do the math and fill out the forms. I'll check your figures—which should make Caitlin happy, that I'm on the case. And then she can sign the damn thing herself."

It sounded reasonable enough. "All right, then."

"Terrific." He was beaming.

She felt warm all over, to have that smile focused on her. Still, she made the effort to keep her tone all business. "What time are we leaving?"

"Barring some unforeseen crisis here, we'll leave High Sierra around five. I'll be flying the Cessna." Aaron owned his own small plane and the Comstock Valley had a tiny, two-runway airstrip. "We should be there by seven, easy, if the weather cooperates. I like that place you found for me last time. See if you can book us in there.''

''The New Venice Inn?''

''Was that it? Fine. Get me the same room as before, if you can. It had a nice big desk in it, and extra phone lines.''

Caitlin had a large, rambling apartment over the Highgrade. But Aaron never stayed with her when he visited. He'd told Celia once that he'd lived with his mother for eighteen full years and that was more than enough for any man.

''And I promise,'' Aaron said, ''that you'll have time to yourself, to be with your friends. So give them a call. Let them know you're coming.''

''Yes, I'll call Jane.'' And Jane would keep after her until she told her all about last night….

Aaron was still giving instructions. ''We'll talk to Caitlin Friday night. Saturday you can get her going on collecting her records for you. Sunday will be all yours. I'll fly out Sunday morning. You can stay over till Monday or Tuesday to finish up with Caitlin, then take a commercial flight home.''

''All right.''

''Celia,'' he said. ''I won't forget you did this for me.''

Her heart started fluttering. *Down girl,* she thought. She warned, ''Just because you've talked me into this doesn't mean your mother is going to go along with it.''

He frowned. ''Shall we get to work, then?''

She got the message: the subject of Caitlin and her taxes was, at least for the time being, closed.

* * *

Celia called Jane that night to say she'd be in New Venice that weekend. "I'll be in Friday. Aaron will need me that evening, and at least some of Saturday. It looks pretty likely that I'll get Saturday evening off. And Sunday should be all mine."

There was a significant silence from the other end of the line.

"Jane? Hull-o."

"I'm here."

"Well. Are you free Sunday?"

"Sure. Are you going to tell me what's going on?"

"About…?"

"I really hate it when you make me bully you to get you to tell me what you know you really *want* to tell me in the first place."

Celia blew out a breath. "Oh, all right."

"So?"

"I told him I love him."

"Omigod. You're serious?"

"You think I would joke about such a thing?"

"No. No, of course not." Jane cleared her throat. "So. You did it. Great. And?"

"He's not interested."

Jane was silent again—but not for long. She let out a small groan. "Oh, Ceil… He said that?"

"Yeah. He tried to be kind. Truly. He was very sweet and very considerate. But in the end, he told me he's not interested and there's no hope he *will* be interested."

"Well," said Jane. Celia thoroughly understood. What else *was* there to say? "And you're still working for him?"

"I volunteered to resign. He convinced me not to—for a while, anyway. We'll see how it goes. And Janey, I'm okay with it. I am. I feel a lot better, having it out there, you know? You were right. Honesty is the best policy."

"Well, of course it is. It's good. A good thing, for you, that you told him. No matter what his response was. And I just have to tell you I am so proud of you."

"Thanks."

"I mean it, Ceil. Congratulations."

"Janey?"

"Yeah?"

"Let's not carry this *too* far. I said I'm okay and I meant it. Congratulations, however, are not in order."

"You're right. Of course you are. So. You'll be home this weekend and I get you Sunday, at least."

"That's right."

"We'll talk more about this then."

"Whatever."

"Celia, are you sure you're okay?"

"Yes, I am. I'm not jumping up and down for joy. But I'm dealing with it. I honestly am."

About ten minutes after she said goodbye to Jane, Jillian called.

Jillian was talking almost before Celia could get the phone to her ear. "Jane just called me."

"What a surprise."

"I am so pleased with this."

"You're pleased."

"You bet."

"And why is that?"

"Because the cards are on the table. Now let him stare at them for a while."

"Jilly, it was a no he gave me. A very clear no. You've heard that word, haven't you? It's the opposite of yes."

"Right, sure. And then he asked you not to quit working for him. If he wasn't interested, that never would have happened. He would have fallen all over himself waving goodbye the minute you offered to resign."

The problem was, that sounded kind of good. Way too good, really. "Jillian. He said no."

"You're not listening. Yes, he said no. And then he begged you not to quit—*and* asked you to fly home with him for the weekend. He—"

"Jilly."

"What?"

"The reason he doesn't want me to quit is that I'm about the best there is at what I do. He knows replacing me won't be easy. I perform all the services of a corporate wife, with none of the messy complications that come with intimacy and sex. I buy great gifts for his girlfriends, I'm a whiz in Word, Excel, Quicken—you name it. I type eighty words a minute and when I take a meeting, I've got my ears open and my mouth firmly shut."

"Well, at least you know your own value in a professional sense."

"I certainly do. As for the other—his taking me home with him—it's nothing romantic."

"How do you know that?"

"I know because he had a bona fide non-romantic reason for asking me to go with him."

"And that is?"

"He needs me to do his mother's taxes."

"Oh, come on."

"It's true. I swear to you. Caitlin drives him crazy every year at tax time."

"But—"

"Jilly, don't make me go into detail about this. There's nothing about it that you really need to know, except I'll be helping out with Caitlin Bravo's taxes and I'm flying home with Aaron this weekend to get started on them."

"All right, all right. You win. It's not romantic."

"Thank you."

"Janey says you're spending Sunday with her."

"That's right."

"I'll be there, too."

"I'd love to see you—and I know that tone of voice. What are you planning?"

"Planning?" Jillian faked guilelessness for all she was worth. "I'm not planning anything. I'll be in New Venice, at Jane's, this weekend. I'm speaking at her bookstore Friday night. 'The New Romantics and the New Millennium.' I'll do hot clothing looks for spring—and relationships, too. Clothes and men. I figure that about covers it."

"I like it—but you *are* planning something. I can hear it in your voice."

"I'll tell you Sunday."

"Jilly—"

"Sunday. I promise. Gotta go now, see you soon."

Chapter Eight

Aaron landed his single engine Turbo Stationair at the Comstock Valley airstrip at a little before seven on Friday night. Celia had booked a rental car. It was waiting for them when they got there. They tossed their suitcases in the trunk and Aaron slid behind the wheel.

His phone rang as he was starting up the car. He looked at the display before he answered it. "It's Caitlin," he said to Celia. "Checking up on me." He spoke into the phone. "What?" He listened, then answered, "Yeah. I'm here. At the airstrip… Yeah, fifteen minutes, tops."

He hung up and they headed for New Venice, a short ride across the valley floor, with the gorgeous, white-capped mountains looming proud above them.

He drove straight to Main Street, which Celia thought looked as homey and welcoming as ever, with its old-fashioned Victorian-style streetlamps and flat-topped two-story buildings, some of brick and some of weathered clapboard. The locust and maple trees that lined the street were still winter-bare, but even in the darkness, Celia could see the bumps along the naked branches that signified spring leaves on the way.

The beauty shop and the post office, the grocery and hardware stores were all closed for the night. But the lights were on at Silver Unicorn Books. Celia smiled to herself. This was Jilly's night: "The New Romantics and the New Millennium."

Aaron turned into the alley between the bookstore and the large white clapboard building that housed the Highgrade Saloon and Café. The parking lot in back was packed, except for a couple of spaces near the door, which were marked, very clearly, Reserved.

Aaron pulled into one of those. The car to the left of them was a handsome, sporty-looking Mercedes, and to the right a dusty celadon-green Porsche. "Looks like Will and Cade are here," he said.

"To wish you a happy birthday?"

"It's a distinct possibility." He scowled. "I smell surprise party. What about you?"

She gave him a nod. "I'm afraid so."

He reached across her and opened her door, his arm brushing the front of her in the process. "There you go."

Celia suppressed a gasp. She could not move. Frantically, she told herself that it had been nothing, the briefest of touches. He didn't even seem to realize he'd done it. Yet, for her, it set off a chain reaction of sensation. Her pulse rocketed into high gear, her stomach went all fluttery and a flush of embarrassment burned on her cheeks. And not only that, her nipples reacted, drawing up instantly into hard little peaks.

''There you go.'' He seemed totally oblivious to her distress.

''Thank you.'' Her voice surprised her, it was so level and calm. She pulled her coat closer around her and got out of that car before he had a chance to notice what his slightest touch could do to her.

He was already out, shutting his door and striding toward the back entrance to the Highgrade. She hesitated for a moment, absently tucking her purse under her arm, hugging her coat around her against the cold northern Nevada night, feeling lost and strange and thoroughly out of her depth.

He paused, turned and glanced back at her, lifting an eyebrow.

He wore one of his beautiful silk suits, a black coat of softest cashmere thrown over it, black calfskin shoes and black leather gloves. He should have looked out of place at the back door of his mother's clapboard saloon. But he didn't. He stood tall and exuded confidence. He was every bit as much at home here as he was striding beneath the glittering lights of High Sierra's mammoth casino.

Her heart ached anew, just to look at him.

I'll get over it, she thought. I'll get over *him*.

''Celia?''

She shoved her own door shut and hustled to catch up with him. When she reached his side, he grabbed the big door handle and pulled the heavy door open, ushering her in ahead of him, letting the door swing shut behind him, which it did automatically with a slow, hydraulic sigh.

A long hallway paneled in knotty pine and lit by two widely spaced, bare ceiling bulbs confronted them, with shut doors at intervals along each side. Celia could hear the ping and clatter of pinball and slots, the whiz and whine of video games. And voices, down that hallway—faint, unrecognizable words, sudden bursts of laughter. She could also smell the smoky, greasy, savory scent of grilling burgers, mingled with the yeasty smell of beer. She hesitated, right there beyond the door.

"My guess is they're all lurking in the bar," Aaron said quietly from behind her. "Go to your right at the end of the hall."

He was quite close—closer than he needed to be, really. She could almost feel the warmth of him at her back.

She should have started walking down that hall.

Instead, she stayed where she was and sent him a glance over her shoulder. "I know where the bar is, Aaron. I grew up here, too, you know."

He didn't seem in any more of a hurry to move on than she was. One corner of his mouth curled lazily in a half-smile. "Oh, that's right. You did, didn't you?"

Was he teasing her? It almost seemed that way.

But why? Why would he do that?

They had an understanding, didn't they? They were going to continue their strictly professional relationship. They would go on as if that conversation in her rooms four nights ago had never taken place.

But it did *take place,* a wiser voice in the back of her mind whispered knowingly. *And we're kidding ourselves if we really think we can go back.*

"Then again," he added, still in that teasing tone, but with a slight edge creeping in, "you didn't really grow up *here,* the way I did. You lived a nice, stable *normal* life—in a real house, with brothers and sisters, a mom *and* a dad."

She turned and faced him fully. "Aaron. Is something the matter?"

He *was* looking at her strangely, his eyes very dark and deep—and shining. "Do you remember," he asked softly, the faint edge that might have been anger fading away again, "oh, you must have been about six or seven? You rode a bike onto Main. It was too big for you. You were struggling along, managing to stay upright. But then you lost it, went over sideways right out in front."

"Eight. I was eight…"

His mouth curled again, in that wonderful lazy half-smile. "You do remember."

"You came to my rescue."

"Let's put it this way, I gave you a hand." He chuckled, a lovely, deep, warm sound. "You didn't say a word. Your eyes were big as saucers. I was one of those crazy Bravo boys and you were terrified of me."

"Oh, I was not." Somehow, she'd sort of backed

up against the wall and he had moved in close. They were only inches apart. She could smell the exciting male scent of him, feel his body heat.

And it was…different…than a minute ago, different than when he'd brushed his arm across her breasts in the car. It was no longer nerve-racking or strange. Now, it seemed very natural to be standing here in the back hall of the Highgrade, flirting with Aaron Bravo.

Flirting? The word repeated itself in her head.

Was that what they were doing?

It sure did feel like it.

"Celia." He clucked his tongue. "Come on. Don't lie to me. You were scared of me."

"Well, all right," she heard herself admitting. "Maybe I was, just a little. But I—"

She didn't get to finish, because Caitlin Bravo's rich and husky contralto interrupted from the other end of the hall. "Aaron, what the hell are you up to back there?"

Aaron's grin changed, grew rueful. But he didn't stop looking right in Celia's eyes. "Go away, Ma. I'm busy."

"Who's that with you?"

Aaron let out a weary breath. "She's not going away," he told Celia in a whisper.

She nodded and whispered back, "You're right. She's not."

"Get on out here, the both of you," Caitlin commanded. She stood dead center at the end of the hall, hands fisted on her hips, the lights of the room behind her outlining her tall, stately figure, a figure that even now, in her fifties, remained shapely enough to turn heads. She wore black jeans so tight it was a wonder she could breathe in them, red cowboy boots and a red Western-style shirt splashed with black sequins that glittered and winked with each breath she took. A red bandana was tied around her neck.

Aaron gestured Celia on with a wave of a black-gloved hand. "After you."

"Gee, thanks."

He made no reply to that, but she could have sworn she heard him chuckle. Celia kept her shoulders back and her head up as she marched toward the raven-haired woman at the end of the hall.

"Ah," said Caitlin, as Celia moved beneath one of the overhead lights. "It's little Celia Tuttle. How are you, sweetie?"

"Just fine, thanks, Mrs.—"

"No." Caitlin put a red-tipped finger to her even redder lips. "You call me Caitlin. Mrs. Bravo sounds like somebody's wife." Caitlin's dark eyes narrowed. "I haven't been any man's wife for over thirty years now—at least not that I realized."

Folks said that the mysterious and long-gone Blake Bravo, the only man Caitlin had ever married, had been the great love of her life. Until recently, they'd all believed he had died years and years ago, leaving Caitlin a widow. But lately, it had come out in the national newspapers that Blake Bravo had lived a lot longer than anyone in New Venice had thought he did, that he had committed the kinds of crimes for which he should have got the gas chamber—or at the very least, been locked up for life. And that after he'd left Caitlin behind forever, he'd married another woman and given *her* a son.

So it didn't surprise Celia that Caitlin seemed pretty ambivalent about being called Mrs. Bravo.

The hall opened out into a big knotty-pine game room: slots, pinball machines and video games on every wall. Aaron and Celia paused there with Caitlin. The whole room was alive with the sounds of the games. On the left wall, by a wide doorway that led to the café and gift shop, stood a long cashier's desk and a big old-fashioned cash register.

A tall, skinny man in a pair of paint-spattered overalls glanced over from one of the pinball machines. "Hey."

"Hey." Aaron nodded in greeting.

The man went back to working his machine, which pinged and bonged with each punch of the buttons.

Caitlin turned for the bar. "Come on, birthday boy. Everyone's waiting to jump out and surprise you." She led them through a wide arch into the bar, which was darker than the game room. Beer signs and a couple of hooded lamps over the twin pool tables provided most of the light.

When Aaron walked beneath the arch, the dark room suddenly erupted with shouts and whistles and raucous catcalls.

Celia scooted to the side and out of the way. Aaron stood where he was, wearing his lazy half-smile, casually removing those black driving gloves. Caitlin headed straight to the battered piano on the far wall, where she slid onto the stool and started beating out

a lively rendition of the birthday song. Everyone—
and there were lots of people there—joined in.

The crowd parted as they reached the last line of
the song and a big freckle-faced woman with carrot-
colored hair worn in two thick braids tied with green
satin ribbons came marching toward Aaron. She carried a white sheet cake ablaze with candles. Celia
knew who she was: Bertha Slider. She'd been
Caitlin's right hand for as long as Celia could remember—some said since before Blake Bravo had faked
his own death in an apartment fire and disappeared
forever from the lives of Caitlin and his three sons.

They sang the last line extra loud. "Happy birthday, dear Aaron, Happy birthday to you." Everybody
shouted and stomped and clapped their hands.

Bertha stopped in front of Aaron. The candles
shone upward, lighting her face to a moon-white
glow. She smiled broadly, revealing small, wide-
spaced teeth. "Make a wish, now, then blow 'em
out."

He tipped his head to the side, frowned—and then
grinned again.

"Blow!" Bertha shouted.

It took him two breaths, but he blew them all out.

After that, he made the first cut. Then he held out
the knife. "Bertha. I think you'd better take over."

"Well, okay, I'll do that, honeybunch." She went
to work cutting up the cake and passing out slices to
all the guests.

Aaron's brothers approached, both tall and handsome: Will dressed in khakis and a cable-knit sweater,
Cade in worn denim with a jacket of soft suede. They

pounded him on the back and called him an old man. He said he wasn't so old he couldn't take on both of them if he had to.

Caitlin left the piano and joined her three sons. "Darlin'," she said to Aaron. "Aren't you hot in that coat?"

"Sure, Ma. A little."

"Hand it over."

He shrugged out of it and she turned for the coat rack in the corner—which was where Celia just happened to be standing.

"Come on, sweetie," said Caitlin. "You take off your coat, too. Stay a while…."

So Celia hung her coat on a hook already layered with other coats. As she turned from the rack, Caitlin reached out and draped an arm across her shoulders. "You have a drink, why don't you, baby doll?" Heady perfume teased Celia's nose—a little strong, yes, but also enticing. Something spicy, with more than a hint of musk.

Celia looked right into Caitlin's black eyes, felt the raw energy of the woman, the will and the strength.

Those dark fingernails squeezed Celia's shoulder. "Sweetie, you with me here?"

"Yes, Caitlin. I'm with you. And I'd love a beer."

"Well, good, then." Caitlin gave her shoulder another squeeze and turned her toward the crowd around the bar.

The party went on until two in the morning, when Caitlin ran everyone out and closed the bar for the night. By two forty-five, there were just the three of them: Caitlin, Aaron and Celia. Cade and Will, like Aaron, had found lodging elsewhere and had already retired to it.

But Aaron hung around, intent on broaching the subject of who would be doing Caitlin's taxes. Since Celia had her own part to play in this scheme, she stayed, too.

Caitlin perched on a barstool and leaned her elbow on the bar, resting her cheek on her fist. "Okay. I guess you're not sleepin' here, right?"

Aaron took the stool next to her. "Right." Just the slightest lift of a brow and Celia got the signal. She slid onto the stool on Caitlin's other side. "Celia booked us at the…" He leaned around his mother and gave Celia a questioning look.

She supplied the name. "The New Venice Inn."

Caitlin turned and looked at her. "Celia sweetie, you are a jewel." Those dark eyes were sparkling.

It occurred to Celia that Caitlin knew exactly what was happening here. She decided a modest smile was all that was required of her at that moment.

Caitlin turned back to her son again. "All right. No cons here, okay? Just lay it right on me."

Aaron said, "Celia's a CPA, did you know that, Ma?"

"Hmm," said Caitlin. She looked at Celia again. "That so?"

Celia nodded.

And Caitlin said, "Well, fine. You convinced me."

Aaron was the one who blinked. "I have?"

"Yep. She's a good girl and she's from town and I like the look of her."

"You do?"

"Yeah. And plus, I get the feeling she'll be a lot easier to get along with than you ever were."

"Well thanks, Ma."

"It's my taxes we're talkin' about here, right?"

"Er, right."

"Well, okay. Celia Tuttle can do my taxes. That's fine with me."

"She's up to something," Aaron said about fifteen minutes later, when they were back in the rental car and on the way to the New Venice Inn.

Celia refrained from rolling her eyes. "She's agreed to do things the way you want them done. What are you worried about?"

"It was too easy. I don't like it. You'll have to keep your eyes and ears open. Watch your back. Understand?"

"Sure. No problem." Celia stared out the windshield at the dark road ahead, thinking that there were times when he really did sound like some Mafia guy.

They reached the inn a few minutes later. It was a charming old Victorian house with lots of cute gables and gingerbread trim. Inside, it had been thoroughly renovated, with marble floors in the bathrooms and big, comfortable queen- and king-sized beds boasting lovely, firm pillow-top mattresses. Aaron had the Rose Suite, which was the largest guest room in the house, on the ground floor. Celia had booked herself a cozy attic room upstairs.

Aaron got their suitcases from the trunk and Celia went to the mailbox in back, where the innkeeper had told her he'd leave the keys. She let them in the back door.

Aaron's room was the first one to the right, near the back entrance. As Celia turned to secure the back door, he set his suitcase on the floor and draped his garment bag over it.

Celia handed him his key. "Here you go." She spoke softly, in order not to disturb any sleeping guests. She already had her little overnighter in one hand. All she needed was the suitcase he had carried in for her. "Thanks for bringing that in. I'll take it now." She reached for it.

He moved it slightly out of her range and whispered, "You're upstairs, you said?"

"That's right."

"I'll carry this up for you."

"Aaron, it's not necessary."

"I don't mind." He turned for the staircase at the front of the long hall that ran through the center of the house.

She watched him walk away from her, wondering what in the world was going on with him—the way he'd flirted with her at the back door of the High-grade. And now, carrying her bag to her room when it wasn't that heavy and there was absolutely no reason she couldn't carry it herself.

He *was* acting strangely.

Tonight, more than once, she'd felt distinctly *not* like his girl Friday and very much like an attractive woman who had caught his interest—his *romantic* interest.

Could it be that Jilly was on to something—that he

really *was* interested, though at first he hadn't let himself admit it?

Aaron must have realized she was still hovering by the door to his room, staring dazedly after him. He paused and glanced back at her. "Are you coming?"

She hurried to catch up.

Chapter Nine

Aaron could hear her soft steps on the stairs behind him.

The past few days, he'd been doing a little... reevaluating.

He'd started to think that maybe he'd been a little hasty in turning Celia down flat.

Though he'd hardly realized what was happening at first, he couldn't help being more and more aware of her as a woman. He supposed it was natural—now she'd told him she cared for him—that he'd take a second look, that he'd see her in a different light.

Not that seeing her in a different light was particularly wise.

She was a damn good secretary and an even better personal assistant, and he was probably a complete idiot to so much as consider messing with that.

But he *was* considering messing with that. He was doing more than considering. He was taking steps.

Now. Tonight. He'd made his decision hours ago, when they were standing in the back hall at the High-grade and he was teasing her about the incident with the bicycle all those years and years ago. He had found himself looking at her soft, plump rosebud of a mouth and accepting the fact that it was a very kissable mouth, a mouth he himself *wanted* to kiss.

He *would* have kissed her, right there, if Caitlin hadn't butted in and ruined the mood.

He reached the second-floor landing. From behind him, Celia whispered, "It's right up there, the attic room."

He stepped aside so she could go ahead, up the final short flight of stairs, to the small third-floor landing with its single door. He mounted the stairs behind her and when he reached her, he waited, so close she brushed against him more than once while she put her key in the lock and pushed the door inward.

She turned to him. "Thanks. Let me—"

"I want to come in, Celia."

She looked eight years old again, staring at him through wide, scared eyes. "Come in?"

"That's right." He started forward. She backed into the room ahead of him and then stood there, be-tween the foot of the bed and door, looking adorably unsure of what she should do next.

She said, cautiously, looking around her, "This is lovely. So cozy, don't you think?"

"Yeah. It's great." And it was, he supposed. If you

went for slanted ceilings and lots of nooks and crannies.

There was a skylight over the bed, a carved armoire for a closet on the wall to the left, next to the bathroom, and a desk against the other wall. He went to the desk, set her suitcase beside it, and flipped on the lamp there. When he turned back to her, she hadn't budged from her position in the middle of the room. She looked very sweet and more than a little bit lost.

He went to her. "Let me take that other bag."

She gave it to him. He carried it over and set it by her suitcase. She still had her coat on, with her black notebook-size purse tucked under her arm.

He returned to her again and teased softly, "You can put your purse down now. I don't think you'll be needing it any time soon."

She took the purse out from under her arm, but instead of setting it aside, she clutched it, hard, against her chest, as if it could protect her from whatever dangerous things he might be planning to do to her.

"Uh. Aaron?"

"Yes?"

"I've got to ask…"

"Go ahead."

"Well, what is this? What are you doing?"

He stepped up even closer. Her eyes got wider. "I'd like you to put the purse down and take off your coat."

"Why?"

He shook his head. "Come on, Celia. The purse. The coat…"

She shut her eyes, dragged in a ragged breath, then let it out hard. "Oh, all right." She tossed the purse on the easy chair, swiftly shrugged out of the coat and threw it on top of the purse. "There. Happy? Now, what's going on?"

He took off his own coat, pitched it over on top of hers.

"Aaron?"

He shrugged. "I wanted to kiss you—earlier, in the back of the Highgrade."

Her face flushed a warm, sweet, tempting pink. "Oh."

He pulled off his gloves, one and then the other. "My mother got in the way. She likes to do that. So I waited for another opportunity to present itself."

"Another opportunity…like now?"

He nodded.

"Oh." She was nodding along with him, looking terrified and excited and very, very kissable.

He tossed the gloves on top of the coat and moved in close to her again. He took her soft chin in his hands, breathed in the sweet, clean scent of her and lowered his mouth to hers.

"We should talk," she said, before his lips actually made contact with hers.

He pulled back enough to meet her eyes. "About what?"

She looked at him, probingly, seeking answers he really didn't have. "About…this. Why you suddenly want to kiss me? Why you told me you weren't interested and you wouldn't *be* interested and then, out of nowhere, tonight…you're interested."

"Can't we just do what comes naturally?" He stroked her hair. It was sleek and smooth and felt good against his palm.

Her breath caught. "Do what comes naturally?"

"Those were my words."

"Well, that depends."

"On?"

"Well, how far, exactly, do you think what comes naturally might go?"

"Celia."

"Hmm?"

"How about if we just start with the kiss?"

"Oh," she said. "Oh, well…"

"And that means?"

"Okay."

"'Okay.' That's a yes?"

She nodded.

Finally.

He lowered his mouth and tasted hers. It was every bit as soft and moist and yielding as he had hoped it might be. He teased at the seam where those soft lips met. She sighed and let his tongue inside. He explored the sweet, slick surfaces in there, wanting her closer, his body already aching and hard with arousal.

He stroked both hands down the sides of her throat, clasped her shoulders and then gathered her to him, wrapping one arm around her and sliding the other one down the smooth curve of her back.

She let out a tiny, lost cry and rubbed herself against him. *Yes,* he thought. *Happy birthday to me….*

He started walking her backward, toward the waiting bed.

She took one step. And then another.

And then she planted her feet and made a protesting noise in her throat. She also started pushing at his shoulders.

He lifted his head. "What?"

That kissable, slightly swollen mouth of hers started moving. "I don't want to do this, Aaron. Not now. Not tonight."

That grated. Seriously. "Wait a minute. Four days ago, you told me—"

"That I'm in love with you. That's right. I did. I am. And you told me no. Never. Forget about it. So I've been working on that. On forgetting about it. And all of a sudden, you're ready to jump into bed with me. I'm not comfortable with that. I'm really not."

He knew he should just turn around and walk out.

Unfortunately, he'd learned something when he kissed her.

He really did want her. He wanted her naked, under him, in a bed.

It was unexpected and inconvenient. But he didn't think turning around and walking out was going to make it go away.

He stepped back. "Celia. What do you want from me? Declarations of love? I'm sorry. As it turns out, I've got some sort of *thing* for you. But love? No. I can't give you that."

She stepped back, too. "A *thing?* You've got a *thing* for me?"

"A yen. An attraction. You get to me. I want you. Am I making myself clear?"

She backed another step and dropped to the end of the bed. She was frowning, considering. Finally, she said, "So you're saying, you don't think you could love me. But you do want to sleep with me."

"I thought I just said that."

"An affair, right, that's what you're after?"

Truth was, he hadn't thought that far.

She took note of his hesitation. "So. You don't know yet, whether you want an affair or not. You just know you want to sleep with me at least once, tonight?"

"Celia…"

She blew out a breath. "And what about our professional relationship?"

He shrugged. "Business is business. I can keep the two separate. Can you?"

She frowned. "I'm not sure."

"So? Give it a try. Play it by ear."

She looked down at her sensible black pumps, then back up at him. "I just, well, I keep thinking about Jennifer."

Jennifer? What did Jennifer have to do with this? "Why should you think about Jennifer?" *He* certainly hadn't, not since the last time he'd seen her, Tuesday, at lunch.

"Well, I just think, if I'm going to have an affair with you, I would like to be the only one—at least for as long as it lasts."

He got the message loud and clear. "You want me to break it off with Jennifer."

"Oh, don't look at me like that. I *like* Jennifer. You know I do. But it wouldn't seem right, sneaking around behind her back."

"Who said a damn thing about sneaking around? Jennifer knows the score. She and I aren't married and she knows we never will be. We have a clear understanding that we don't own each other, that we're both free to do as we please."

"Oh, Aaron…" She was shaking her head, looking at her shoes again. "I wouldn't like that, you sleeping with both of us. It would just seem icky to me."

"Icky."

"Yes. Icky. Sorry, but that's the way I feel. I can live without your loving me—obviously. You don't, and here I am, still breathing. But if you think you want to get something going with me, then you'll have to say goodbye to Jennifer first."

Chapter Ten

Jilly threw back her head and let out a loud bray of laughter. "You *said* that?"

Fierce approval shone in Jane's eyes. "Well, I think it's terrific. She laid it on the line with him. As in, 'Say goodbye to Jennifer or it's not going to be happening between the two of us.' More women ought to do that. They'd lead much happier lives."

It was Sunday night and they were sitting on the blue rug at Jane's in front of a cozy fire, all comfy in lush piles of pillows, drinking green tea with honey and eating biscotti left over from the refreshments at Jillian's bookstore appearance Friday night.

Jillian was suddenly thoughtful. "I should have said something like that to Benny, way back when. But then again, Benny was such a hound. It probably wouldn't have done any good. What's that old saying? 'You knew I was a snake when you brought me into the house'?"

"Well." Jane paused for a sip of her tea. "We live and learn, don't we?" Her gaze shifted away just the tiniest bit. Celia knew she was probably thinking of her own disastrous marriage.

Jillian leaned toward Celia. "So? What happened next?"

"He said goodnight and left."

"That's *all?*"

"Pretty much. He flew his plane back to Las Vegas yesterday afternoon. I drove him to the airstrip."

"And?"

"And nothing. He was polite and professional. Neither of us said a thing about what had happened the night before. I gave him his birthday present. He opened it on the way to the airstrip."

"It was?"

"An antique silver money clip. He said, 'Thank you, Celia. Very much.'"

Jillian groaned. "Girl, you amaze me. Nerves of steel."

Celia pondered the tea leaves at the bottom of her china cup. "The hardest thing for me was telling him in the first place. There's just nothing that can be as tough as that." She looked from one true friend to the other. "It's funny, when you work with someone as closely as I've worked with Aaron. You learn things about them. You learn...what they are. Deep down. He doesn't have the faintest idea how to make a lasting relationship with a woman. Men and women, together, forming permanent bonds, well, that's strange and scary to him. But then again, he's always honest with women about where he stands, about what they can expect from him.''

Jillian gestured broadly, both palms up. ''Which is?''

Celia looked in her cup again, then back up at Jillian. ''Lots of glamour and good times. If you're with Aaron, you'll eat at the best tables in the finest restaurants and he'll shower you with fabulous gifts. It's not a bad deal, really, as long as you're not in the market for anything permanent.''

''Which you *are*,'' Jane reminded her softly.

Celia set her cup carefully on the fireplace bricks. ''That's true. I am.'' She settled back into her pile of pillows. ''And it's very likely I won't get what I'm after. I can accept that. And I know *he* accepts what I told him Friday night. Aaron Bravo may not be the marrying kind. But he has true integrity, deep down, where it counts. Maybe he'll break it off with Jennifer, and maybe he won't. But he won't make another move on me until—and unless—he has.''

Aaron shifted the bouquet of flowers to his left hand and rang the doorbell with his right.

A minute later, Jennifer opened the door. ''Ah,'' she said, granting him her gorgeous smile. ''Flowers. I like flowers...'' Then she looked closer, into his eyes, and a frown drew down the corners of her full mouth. ''But that serious face of yours, I'm not so sure about that.'' She reached out, wrapped her slim hand around his sleeve. ''What else you got, *caro?*''

Gently, he shook off her grip and reached in his pocket. He pulled out an oblong blue velvet box.

She took the box, opened it, sighed, and closed the lid. "It's beautiful."

"I thought you'd like it."

"And you'd better come in, I think." She took his arm again and pulled him into her apartment.

They'd moved into the kitchen to microwave a bag of popcorn when Jane asked, "So how's it going with Caitlin?"

"You won't believe this. It's going great."

Jillian made a scoffing sound. "You're kidding, right?"

"No, honestly, she's been completely cooperative, gave me everything I needed. I'm meeting with her once more tomorrow, to get a few more figures she didn't have for me yesterday. Then I'm on my way back to Vegas. I'll fill out all the forms and pass it on to Aaron and that's it. I'm done."

Jillian leaned against the counter and crossed her arms over the breasts that had been the envy of all the girls at New Venice High. "I thought you said she drove Aaron crazy every year at tax time."

"She does. She has. And up till now, every accountant he's found for her, she's fired. But not me. I've got no problem with her. As I said, for me, she's cooperative. She gets me what I need when I ask for it. She's actually very well organized. And if you think about it, she'd have to be. The woman *has* been running her own business for over three decades and doing a darn good job of it, too. My theory is, Aaron expects her to drive him crazy—and she obliges him. It's part of the way they relate to each other. I, on the other hand, don't have any family relationship stuff going on with her.''

"*And* you're a woman," Jillian added. "I'll bet all the other accountants he found for her were men.''

"Now you mention it, that's right. At least in the past three years, since I've been working for him.''

"Hmph," said Jillian, "I thought so.''

"Plus, she likes me. She pretty much said so Friday night.''

"Said what," Jane demanded, "specifically?''

"She said, and I quote, 'She's a good girl and she's from home and I like the look of her.'''

Jillian let out a gleeful little squeal. "Oh, I love it.''

"She calls me baby doll and sweetie.''

Even Jane chuckled at that. By then, the popcorn was popping like mad. The three fell silent and stared into the window of the microwave. The bag turned in a stately circle, inflating as the kernels within exploded.

Finally, Celia said, "Aaron thinks Caitlin's up to something, since she was so agreeable about my taking over on the tax front.''

"And what do *you* think?" asked Jane.

"I don't know. Could be. It's hard to tell with someone like Caitlin. On the one hand, she's so volatile. Always the center of attention, never afraid to say what's on her mind. On the other hand, well, who *really* knows what goes on inside that woman's head?''

Jillian wiggled her eyebrows. "I heard Hans is no more."

Jane turned and got a bowl down from the cupboard. "Well, he hasn't been in the bookstore lately, I can tell you that." The popping sounds had slowed. Jane set the bowl on the counter. She punched a button at the base of the microwave. The popcorn stopped turning and the door swung wide. Jane grabbed the bag, held it over the bowl and tore it open. "Ouch!" she cried as the fat, buttery kernels tumbled out. "That is *hot.*"

They returned to the front room and their piles of pillows. Celia stuck a big handful of popcorn in her mouth and chomped away. "Umm. So good…" She was reaching into the bowl again when she realized her friends were staring at her. She pulled her hand back. "What?"

Slowly and knowingly, Jillian smiled.

Celia understood. "All right. I know that smile. It's about what you're planning, right? What you just couldn't talk about on the phone the other day?"

Jillian said, "Even Jane agrees with me now."

Celia glanced Jane's way and got a quick nod of confirmation.

Jillian continued, "You've told him how you feel about him. Jane is very proud of you."

"Oh, yes," said Jane. "I am. So proud."

"And now it's time you took some of *my* advice."

Celia got the picture. "Hair, lipstick and wardrobe. Right?"

"Exactly. We are flying down to Vegas next weekend."

"We?"

"Jane and me. You will save Saturday for us. All day Saturday. Is that clear? I'm pulling a few strings, and I expect you to make yourself completely available. Because I'm putting the best in the business to work on you. Hair. Makeup. Nails. And then shopping…"

Celia thought of all those gray clothes she'd dug out of her closet last Monday night. If Aaron did say goodbye to Jennifer, Celia wouldn't mind having something that wasn't gray to wear when he next attempted to seduce her. "Will I be a redhead?"

"You want to be a redhead?"

"You know, Jilly, I do. I really do."

"Good answer. Is that a commitment? You'll give us all day Saturday, and no backing out?"

"Yes. All day Saturday. I promise. I do."

"Triple Threat," said Jane, raising her teacup.

"Triple threat," Celia and Jillian responded in unison. They raised their cups and drank.

"Well, baby doll," said Caitlin. "You got everything you need?"

"I think so." Celia gathered up the pile of papers Caitlin had given her that day. She tapped them on the edge of Caitlin's big green metal desk and slipped them into the briefcase she'd brought with her from her room at the New Venice Inn. "I'll fill out all the forms, pass everything on to Aaron to check over, and then he'll get it back to you. Should be ready in a week or so."

"Thanks, sweetie, I—" The phone rang. Caitlin put up a red-tipped index finger. "One minute?"

"Sure."

Caitlin picked up the phone. "Highgrade." She listened and then she sighed and sat back in her swivel chair. "Umm." She listened some more, lightly touching one corner of her red mouth and then the other, wiping nonexistent smudges away. "Hans," she said at last, her smoky voice infinitely tired and wise. "Hans. No...I can't...I mean it. And I've gotta go now. Goodbye, my darlin'." She hung up the phone, the purple spangles on her black shirt shimmering and winking as she heaved a second sigh. "Young men. They have way too much energy..."

Not sure what she ought to say, Celia nodded too hard. "Oh, well. I'd imagine so."

Caitlin sat forward and folded her hands on the desktop. "Now. Let's talk about what really matters."

Celia had a sinking feeling. Was Caitlin getting to it then, to the thing Aaron had warned her about, the reason she needed to be watching her back? "Uh. Sure. Go ahead. Talk."

Caitlin's black eyes shone now with a probing light. "I am with you here, you get me?"

"Uh...?"

"I'm sayin' I saw you with Aaron the other night, back there in the shadows at the end of my hallway. I know what's going on. And I like it. I like it a lot." She picked up a pencil, tapped it on the desk once, then tossed it down. "And I'm not sayin' a word to him, either, about what I know. I'm stayin' out of it, one hundred percent. I'm lettin' you play this hand, just play it out your own way. 'Cause I got a good feelin' 'bout you, baby doll. I truly do. I'd put my money on you in this game. And I'd come out a winner, too.''

"Well," said Celia, for lack of anything better, "thanks."

Caitlin smiled. "You need anything, you can come to me. Anytime."

"Well. Okay. I'll remember that."

"Anything. I mean that. Anything. Anytime."

Celia was at her desk Tuesday morning when Aaron entered the office suite.

She looked up, their gazes locked for perhaps two seconds, and then he smiled. An all-business smile. "I'm surprised. You're back so soon."

She produced a smile as professional as his, though her blood raced in her veins and her heart pounded madly. "I had everything I needed from your mother. I decided I might as well get back to work."

He slanted her a doubtful look. "You're telling me that she didn't give you any trouble?"

"That's right. No problems. I'll crunch the numbers and fill out the forms. In a few days, I'll have it all ready for you."

"You're serious? And you got no indications from her of anything else going on, anything…suspicious she might be up to?"

She decided to finesse that one. "It all went smoothly. I have nothing to report. Except…mission accomplished."

"Well. I don't know what to say. Thank you, Celia."

"You're welcome, Aaron."

"And I'm glad you're back early. Managers' meeting this morning at ten-thirty. I'd like you there with me."

"Will do."

"Great. Give me ten minutes, we'll go over the calendar."

"Fine. Ten minutes it is."

Strictly professional.

That was how they kept things. Tuesday went by, and Wednesday and Thursday.

Aaron never said a word about what had happened between them the night of his birthday party. All physical contact had stopped, too. He no longer brushed her hand or her arm in casual acknowledgement when she brought him coffee or handed him a file.

And that was just fine with her. She didn't want any more of those little heartbreaking, meaningless touches from him.

He could touch her for real. Or he could keep his hands to himself.

He never mentioned Jennifer.

And Celia didn't ask.

The next move, the way she saw it, had to be his.

It wasn't easy, waiting. Wondering. Hoping. Jillian was wrong. She didn't really have nerves of steel.

More than once, she caught herself hanging on the verge of inquiring out of nowhere, "So, tell me.

How's Jennifer? Did you happen to break it off with her?''

But she managed *not* to say that, somehow. Whenever she got close, she'd think of Caitlin, leaning toward her across that big green desk, spangles glittering, all that impossibly black, black hair gleaming in the hard light from the ceiling fixture above. "I got a good feelin' 'bout you, baby doll. I truly do. I'd put my money on you in this game. And I'd come out a winner, too...."

And after Caitlin, she remembered her friends, who were coming that weekend to give her the full treatment, to enhance her makeup, change her hair, help her get into some brighter clothes. If she was going to end up throwing herself at him, she wanted to be wearing something stunning when she did it.

And speaking of stunning, what was it with her underwear? It was all in pale blues and pinks—and yes, all right, gray. It was good quality, and a lot of it was satin, some of it even trimmed with lace.

But when Aaron Bravo saw her panties, she was determined that those panties would be red. Or purple. Or black. Some strong, assertive color, something naughty and bold.

Friday, she kept waiting for him to say he would need her on Saturday. She was all prepared for that, to tell him she was sorry, but she had *plans* for Saturday, plans that she simply was not willing to change.

But he never asked. So she never to got to tell him how she wasn't available. He left the office at four-thirty.

"Have a good weekend, Celia," he said on his way out.

She did not look up from her computer screen. "I will, thank you, Aaron. See you Monday."

And he was gone.

Celia listened to the door closing behind him and stared blindly at her computer screen, imagining him rushing to Jennifer's place. Oh, yes. She could just see it: the gorgeous, kind-hearted showgirl greeting him at the door wearing nothing but a red sequined thong, a see-through chiffon robe and that unforgettable smile.

Celia blinked. "Enough of that silliness," she told herself firmly and forced her mind back to the columns of figures in front of her.

Jane and Jillian got into McCarran at seven that night. Celia was waiting for them. Jane said she wanted to cook at least a couple of meals during their visit. So they stopped off at the supermarket and picked up the things she'd need. Then Celia took them back to her rooms at High Sierra so they could drop off their bags and freshen up a little.

For dinner that night, Celia took them to Casa D'Oro, right there in High Sierra, where the fare was a nice blend of Mexican and California cuisines. Once they'd eaten, they returned to Celia's apartment. By eleven, they were saying goodnight. And at seven, they were up and dressed. Jane served them French toast as only Jane knew how to make it—with whole wheat bread, heavy on the cinnamon, fresh blueberries on top.

Jillian had the day all planned. Celia was due for hair at nine, and a makeup consultation at eleven. At one, they all took a break for lunch.

And then they spent the afternoon at the best and most exclusive shops Las Vegas had to offer. They put some serious stress on Celia's gold card.

"You can afford it," said Jillian with a shrug. "Aaron Bravo may not be husband material, but I know he pays you well. Might as well get some mileage out of those hefty paychecks."

Celia didn't argue. What was to argue about? Jilly spoke the truth. And no matter what happened with Aaron, well, at least now Celia knew what it felt like to be a redhead. That alone, was worth all the money she'd spent.

That night, they went over to Bellagio to catch one of the shows there. Sunday morning, Jane made her famous huevos Californios, which, besides eggs, included salsa, sour cream, avocado and hot, soft flour tortillas.

"With food like this, who needs sex?" Jillian wondered aloud.

"Jilly," said Jane. "It is balance in all things for which we strive."

Celia drove her friends back to the airport at eleven so they could catch separate flights. Then she returned to High Sierra, went straight to her rooms and finished preparing Caitlin's taxes.

She wore her new red satin teddy to bed.

"A redhead," Aaron said Monday morning when he entered the office suite and found the "new" Celia sitting at her desk.

He watched her straighten her shoulders and smile—a smile that was half nervous and half naughty. "That's right. Do you like it?"

"I do. It suits you." And it did. Not carrot-colored, not auburn. A truer kind of red, rich and spicy—like cinnamon. Or maybe paprika....

"Aaron?" she prompted.

He realized he'd been standing there staring at her. He shook himself, demanded gruffly, "Ten minutes?"

"Of course."

He went into his office, where he found his mother's completed tax return waiting on his desk. He picked up the forms. And then he set them down.

He punched a button on the phone in front of him. "Celia."

"Yes?"

"I wonder if you could come in here right now?"

Twenty seconds later, she stood in front of his desk, with her notebook in one hand and her miniature recorder in the other.

He said, "That's a new suit, too, isn't it?"

She looked down at the snug-fitting suit—a warm, spicy red, like her hair, like her soft, oh-so-kissable lips—and back up at him. "Yes, Aaron. It is."

A glass desktop did have its advantages. He let his gaze travel down, all the way down. The pencil-thin skirt ended right above her pretty knees. Her shoes, which matched the suit, had skinny high heels and very pointed toes—not her usual practical pumps, no not at all.

"Celia, what have you been up to?"

She didn't answer—at first. Not until he raised his gaze and met those hazel eyes. They shone bright with challenge—and apprehension, too. "That sounds like a personal question."

"Probably because it *is* a personal question."

"I don't think we should get into that—not now, not in the office."

"Would you care to suggest a different time, then?"

"Uh. Yes. I would. How about tonight, seven o'clock, my rooms?"

"I have a better idea."

She gulped. "You do?"

"Let's take a couple of hours off and go to *my* rooms. Right now."

She almost dropped her tape recorder. "Oh!" She caught it just before it hit the edge of the desk.

He hid a smile. "Nervous?"

"Yes. I am." She turned and set both the notebook and the recorder on the chair behind her, then made herself face him once more. He saw the small shiver that traveled through her. And it pleased him. "Very nervous," she whispered, more to herself, it seemed, than to him.

He asked again, careful to be gentle this time, "Will you come to my rooms with me?"

"Er, right now?"

"Yes, Celia. Right now."

"But is that advisable? I mean, during working hours?"

"Celia—" His cell phone started bleating. He took it out of his pocket, glanced at the display, then switched it off and dropped it to his desk.

A frown formed between her smooth brows. "Shouldn't you answer that?"

"It's nothing important."

"But—"

"Celia. I am the boss. I set the hours."

"Well, um, that's right. I suppose you do."

Her face was almost as red as her hair. He found her enchanting. He'd been waiting for a week for some kind of sign from her, some indication that she would welcome another move, if he made it.

He said, "Look. I thought...the hair, that new suit, those sexy shoes..." He waved a hand. "I'm reading them as an invitation. Have I got it all wrong?"

"Uh, no. No, you haven't. You have got it very right." A sweet, high laugh burst from her. She clapped her hand to her mouth to stop it—and blushed all the harder.

He let his own smile show. "So? What do you say?"

"Yes," she said, adorable and firm. "I say, yes. Let's take two hours off and spend them in your rooms."

Chapter Eleven

Aaron's suite was in a different tower than the one that housed the office complex. They rode down in one elevator and walked through the casino, ablaze as always with glittering light, alive with bells and whistles and electronic buzzing, with the clattering of coins, and the clicking whirr of roulette wheels.

People recognized Aaron, of course. Those people nodded and muttered respectful greetings. Aaron always nodded back.

To Celia, it felt…strange, unreal. Like a dream. They walked close together, but not touching. Surely to any casual observer, they were just what they'd always been: the boss and his assistant, en route from the office tower to meet a manager or a vice president or one of the board members—or maybe some major high roller. A whale—like Dennis Rodman, or the oil-rich sultan of a certain Middle Eastern country. But whatever their destination, whoever they might be meeting, surely all assumed them to be intent on business as usual.

Could anyone tell, by looking at them, that they were headed for his private suite to spend a couple of hours crawling all over each other, naked in his bed?

No way, Celia decided.

No one would guess.

Oh, eventually, she knew, if they did this more than once or twice, word would get around that the boss and his assistant shared more than a professional relationship. One of the maids or some other employee would spot them going into or out of his or her rooms. There would be whispering. The story would spread.

But not yet. No one had a clue yet.

She kept half-expecting someone to stop them, to pull Aaron aside with some question or other, some issue that simply could not wait. She kept thinking, *this isn't really happening, this is just a daydream, just a crazy, impossible fantasy. I'm really sitting at my desk, staring blindly at my computer screen. Any minute now, I'm going to snap out of it.*

But she didn't snap out of it. And no one stopped them. They left the casino and proceeded down two intersecting hallways where the floors were marble, crystal chandeliers hung from the high ceilings and the walls were papered in gilded leaf patterns on a ground of antique gold. They approached another set of elevators. One of them was open, a uniformed operator perched on a stool inside.

"Mr. Bravo," said the operator.

"Miles." Aaron nodded, as he'd nodded at all the others on their way here.

And right then, for the first time since the night that he'd kissed her, Aaron touched her. He laid his hand, so lightly, at the small of her back, the way a man will do. He was ushering her onto the car—and also, in a subtle way, laying claim to her. A shiver of pure arousal coursed through her. And the feeling of unreality shattered.

This *was* happening. Not a daydream. *True.*

She stepped into the car, sparing a quick, polite smile for Miles. The door—which was mirrored in gold-veined glass—slid shut. And there she was, looking at herself, red-haired in a red suit, a red clutch tucked neatly under her arm, standing next to Aaron Bravo. So very disorienting, to see how calm she looked on the outside, while inside she was all tangled up in yearning, in a strange and wonderful admixture of heat and jitters and fear and glorious, giddy, light-headed joy.

They went up, slowly at first, then kicking into high speed. In less than a minute, there they were. On the top floor. The door slid wide. She looked beyond and saw that the elevator opened directly into the foyer of an apartment.

Aaron took her elbow. Heat sizzled where he touched her, radiating outward, setting her whole body on fire.

"Thank you, Miles."

The operator nodded. Aaron and Celia stepped out into the entrance hall, a large, high-ceilinged room where morning sunlight poured down on them through a huge round skylight. Celia looked up, saw twining flowers and leaves etched into the dome-shaped glass. The desert sky, seen between the frosty patterns of leaf and petal, was pastel blue and cloud-less.

Behind them, the door to the elevator whispered shut.

Celia noted the iron-framed glass entry hall table, the simple, white-shaded lamps, the walls that were a color between green and khaki and beige, the blood-red freesias in a tall glass vase. Twin Ionic pillars and a single, pulled-back silk portiere of a lustrous brown framed the entrance to the living room.

It was all so like him. Understated. And yet some-how theatrical to the core.

"You're quiet," he said.

She turned to him. "I...one minute I feel certain this can't be happening. And then the next, I realize, my God, it *is*."

He touched her again—a miracle, each time he did that—his lean hand brushing a caress along the line of her hair at her temple. "Is that a backing-out re-mark?"

She captured his hand. He let her do that. It felt so good, his palm touching hers. "No. I promise. It's not."

He twined his fingers with hers, then pulled her into him, placing their joined hands at the small of her back, cupping her chin with the warm fingers of his other hand.

Slowly those fingers moved, sliding downward, caressing her throat. He lowered his mouth so it hovered no more than an inch from hers. Her eyelids felt heavy. She longed to just let them drift shut.

But some part of her couldn't quite do that. She couldn't help feeling that certain things had to be said first.

He pulled back a fraction. "What?"

She made a small noise of protest, of avoidance.

His arm tightened around her. "Go ahead. Say it."

She struggled to find the right words. There didn't seem to be any.

He touched her nose, so lightly, traced her cheekbone, and the line of her brow. "This is about Jennifer. Right?"

She closed her eyes then, not terribly proud of herself that she just had to ask him, she just *had* to know. "Right."

She felt the brush of his lips across her own—once, and then again. With a hungry sigh, she pressed herself closer to him. She could feel how he wanted her. That thrilled and excited her—and made her pretty nervous, too. "Oh, Aaron…"

He released her and pulled back. "Okay, let's get it over with. What about Jennifer?"

She dragged in a ragged breath and opened her eyes. He was watching her, studying her. It took a real effort to make herself meet that probing gaze directly. "Well, I know that you must have ended it with her…."

He was smiling, but his eyes were dark as midnight. "How do you know that?"

She gave a small, embarrassed cry. "Oh, don't tease me. Please."

He studied her face some more. Then he shrugged. "You're right. I ended it with her. A week ago Sunday. I went to her apartment, gave her flowers and a diamond bracelet. She invited me in. I stayed for about ten minutes. Just long enough to tell her goodbye. I haven't seen her since then."

He must have read what she was thinking in her eyes, because he added, ruefully, "Yes. It's true. I went out and bought the damn bracelet myself."

That did make her smile. "Good for you." She felt her smile fading as she couldn't help but wonder when she would be the one getting the diamonds.

He said, as if, again, he saw into her mind, "It always ends in diamonds, Celia."

That made her so sad. She looked down. But he wouldn't allow that. He put a finger under her chin, guiding her face up so she was looking at him again. "I'm the son of a murdering bigamist and a woman who, to this day, has never settled on one man. I don't *do* marriage. I have sense enough to know the things I'll never get right. You know that, you *understand* that?"

Her throat closed up so words wouldn't come. But she did make herself nod.

"Then we're clear about this? You don't expect me to be someone I'm not?"

She swallowed, shook her head.

He chuckled. "No, you're not clear, or no, you don't expect me to be someone I'm not?"

She wrinkled her nose at him. "Yes. I'm clear. I don't expect you to be a person you're not."

"Okay then." He wrapped his arm around her again and pulled her body into his. "Anything else?"

She came up against his chest. It felt warm and hard and absolutely lovely. "Uh. No. I'd say that's pretty much it."

"Then, will you let me kiss you now?"

"Oh, yes." She lifted her mouth and closed her eyes. "Please do."

She sighed as his lips met hers, her foolish heart lifting, her body going soft and needful, her pulse pounding out his name.

The kiss was long and wet and very thorough. Celia gave herself up to it, gladly, with joy.

When he lifted his head, his mouth looked swollen. One corner of it kicked up in that characteristic lazy half-smile of his. "You can put your purse down now, Celia." He gestured with a flick of his head. "There. On the glass table, by the vase of flowers…"

She had her arms around his neck by then, and clutched the purse in her left hand. "Uh, no. I'll just…take it to the bedroom with us, if that's okay with you."

Now he lifted a dark brow. "Some reason you need it?"

"Um, yes, there is."

"And that is?"

"Well…." She cleared her throat, suddenly embarrassed and wishing she wasn't, wanting to be more…sophisticated about this.

"What's in the bag, Celia?"

She told him. "Contraception."

"Ah." Those eyes of his gleamed at her, blue as Lake Tahoe at its deepest point. "Contraception. In your purse?"

"That's right."

He laughed then. She felt the deep, pleasured rumble against her heart. "Celia. You never cease to amaze me. A model of efficiency. Ready for anything, as always."

She had gone out and bought the condoms a week ago. She'd intended to be ready—if and when. "Well. Hope springs eternal, as they say."

He scanned her face, his gaze wonderfully avid, as if he couldn't get enough of looking at her. "You *are* charming…."

"Why, thank you."

"And so pretty."

"Keep talking. I do sincerely like what you're saying."

But he had fallen silent. He cupped her left shoulder with his right hand, the gesture, somehow, stunning in its intimacy. Then his fingers moved.

She slanted him a suspicious look. "What are you doing?"

Her suit had a short semi-wrap jacket that buttoned on the left side. As she watched, he freed that button. And then the next one. There were only five in all.

"Aaron."

"Um?" Button number three gave way.

"I think we should go on to your bedroom now."

Oops. There went number four. She could see the scrap of bright red lace beneath—her lovely, naughty, meant-for-seduction new bra. He slid that last button free and gently edged the facing aside. "Celia, I am liking what I see here."

"Well, good." She grabbed that naughty hand of his, turned and started for the living room. "Where's the bedroom?"

He wouldn't budge. "Don't you think it's nice right where we are, under the skylight?"

She looked up. "The skylight I can live with—but not that elevator over there."

"No one will disturb us."

"You think."

"Celia—"

"The bedroom, Aaron. Please."

He was grinning. "I like you with your jacket unbuttoned and that gorgeous red lace peeking out underneath, with that just-been-kissed look on your face and a blush on your cheeks…"

"The bedroom?"

"I have to ask. To what do I owe all this red?"

She stopped tugging on his hand and simply glared at him.

Aaron relented.

Yes, he would have thoroughly enjoyed undressing her beneath the skylight.

But if she worried the whole time about Miles coming back, it would ruin her pleasure. He didn't want that. He decided he'd take her where she wanted to go.

Sparing one last rueful glance at the skylight above, he moved to take the lead. "All right. This way." He pulled her through the living room and down a hallway to the room at the end.

She hesitated in the doorway. "Oh. It's all white…"

It was, for the most part. He had a wide white bed with a white woven cotton headboard, a pair of white marble nightstands, one to either side, and a white art-deco-inspired limestone fireplace. No dressers or bureaus, since the room contained two walk-in closets fitted with all the drawers and shelves he could possibly need. There was also a sitting area, with a deep white couch and two matching easy chairs, a glass coffee table between them. And there were etched-glass mirrors, in varying shapes, here and there along the walls. Aaron liked mirrors, liked the way they added space, they way they glittered, amplifying the light.

As it happened, even the flowers on the nightstand to the left of the bed were white right then—calla lilies.

He led her over to the end of the bed. "Have a seat." She did, demurely, clutching her purse with its crucial load of condoms, her red hair and red clothes all the more vivid against all the white, her jacket gaping open in a most alluring way.

He felt…very young, suddenly. A boy with his first woman, starving to have her.

He turned from her, to pace himself. It was always better, when he wanted something badly, to take it easy, draw out the pleasure, to make himself go slow.

With his back to her, he shrugged out of his own jacket and removed his tie, tossing them over one of the white chairs. Then he went to work on his cuff links, dropping them into a carved ivory dish that waited on the glass table between the couch and the chairs.

He knew he couldn't stay turned away for too long. She was just insecure enough that she might take it all wrong. So after he'd unbuttoned his shirt and tossed it on the chair, too, he faced her again.

She looked up at him, eyes wide, mouth slightly parted—yearning. Yet unsure.

He undid his belt and slid it off, then went to the white ottoman not far from the bed. He sat, began removing his shoes. "So…"

Her sweet face went eager, and so hopeful. "Um?"

He wanted to take away that jacket, the scrap of lace beneath, to see her breasts, to touch them….

Soon.

But not yet.

"I think you should tell me what you've been up to."

"I should?"

He nodded, set his shoes beside the ottoman. "That suit, the hair, the shoes…" He went to work on his socks.

"Well, my friends came, this weekend. Jane and Jillian…"

He dropped the socks across the shoes. "That would be Jane Elliott, whose uncle, J. T. Elliott, was once the sheriff and is now the mayor."

"That's right."

"And Jillian's last name is Diamond. She's an image consultant, right?"

"That's it. Very good." A smile quivered across her mouth. He wanted to kiss it, that mouth, to taste that trembling smile.

And he would.

Soon...

He stood. Her eyes widened. He looked down at his own hands as he unbuttoned his slacks and casually stepped out of them. He put them with rest of his clothes.

All that was left was his silk boxer shorts. He looked at Celia again. "So your friends came. And the image consultant offered a little advice...."

She nodded. "That's right. Hair, nails, you name it."

"Ah," he said, slipping the waistband of his boxers over his erection and stepping out of them as he had the slacks, letting them drop to the floor.

He stood tall, facing her. She made a sweet, scared noise low in her throat. Her eyes were so big, they seemed to take up her whole face.

He wondered, at that moment, if she might be a complete innocent. It seemed a little difficult to believe. She was in her late twenties. Not many women were virgins at that age—not in his experience, anyway. Truth was, he couldn't think of a one. However, if Celia just happened to be the last of the late-twenty-something virgins....

Well, he'd have to rethink this situation. He'd come to accept the fact that he wanted her. A lot. He was standing in front of her naked and way too eager to do what came naturally.

But he didn't make love to virgins.

"Celia."

"Um?"

"I have to ask this."

"Uh, what?"

"Is this your first time?"

She stared at him blankly. Then comprehension dawned. "Oh. With a man, you mean."

"Right."

"Uh. No. There was someone—well, two someones, actually. First, Derek Pauley, in high school. Remember him? He's still in the Comstock Valley, a farmer. Like his father was before him. Dairy farmers, remember? With very happy cows. Holsteins, I think they were, black and white with those big, soft eyes and—"

"Hold it." He gave her a smile. "That's all the info I need for right now."

"Oh. Well. Of course. Sure…"

When her voice trailed off, he said, very softly, "I just want to be certain you're okay."

"Oh. Oh, yes. I'm fine." She nodded madly, clutching that red purse for all she was worth. "Just so nervous, all of a sudden. It…well, this is really happening, you and me, here, in your bedroom, isn't it?"

"Yes, Celia. It is."

He went to her, half expecting her to jump up as he approached, to back away—or even bolt from the room. But she held her ground, there, on the bed.

He reached out a hand, carefully, and traced the line of that crimson hair with an index finger. "Maybe," he suggested quietly, "we can get what we need from that purse and then you can let go of it."

Her mouth quivered. "Um…"

"Is that a yes?"

She nodded again, this time more slowly.

He turned his hand over and waited. She blinked, twice, then she opened the purse, dug around in it, and came up with three condoms. She put the condoms in his open hand.

"The purse, too."

She handed it over. He went to the left nightstand, set the purse down on the outer edge of it and the condoms closer in.

When he got back to her, she stood. "I—"

"Shh…" He reached for her, slowly, easing his fingers beneath the warm fall of that shining hair, cupping the back of her neck.

She tipped her mouth up to him, whispered, "Aaron…"

"What?"

"Oh." She was frowning, as if whatever she'd meant to tell him had somehow escaped her. "Uh. Nothing."

He brushed his mouth against hers, "Just 'Aaron'?"

"That's all."

"You're sure?"

Her frown deepened. "You are teasing me."

"Maybe."

"You ought to stop that. It just makes me more nervous."

"Stop that and…?"

"Kiss me."

He brushed her lips with his again. "Kiss you?"

"That's right, Aaron. Kiss me. Now."

How could he refuse such a sweet command?

And why would he want to?

He settled his mouth against hers and he gave her just what she wanted, lightly at first, then deepening it a little, but being careful not to pull her into his naked body. She sighed, opening to his questing tongue. Her mouth was silky. Warm. Good. He tasted her to the limits of his control.

At the point where he knew he would grab her and crush her close, he lifted his head. Her eyes drifted open, the pupils wide, drugged with the promise of pleasure.

Yeah. She was relaxing, letting go, letting the nervousness fade away. He could feel the tension easing from the tendons at the back of her neck.

He let his hand go roaming, around to the front of her. "Soft," he said. "Touchable. Nice…"

He slid both hands between the open sides of the red jacket, guiding it over her shoulders and down her arms. She squirmed a little, her arms trapped behind her. He paused in the act of undressing her, his hands holding her arms, the jacket falling halfway down her back. He paused and he stole another long, drugging kiss.

This time, he dared to rub his chest against her. Her breasts were small and high and the red lace of that sexy bra was scratchy, arousingly so. She moaned into his mouth and arched her back, pressing harder, closer....

He raised his head again and he helped her to pull her arms from the sleeves of the jacket. He tossed it away, not caring where it landed. Then he wrapped one arm around her, to steady her, and with the other, he carefully guided the lacy cups of that bra out of the way, revealing two sweet, delicate white breasts tipped with coral-colored nipples.

"So pretty..." He lowered his head and captured one hard little bead.

She moaned and clutched his head. He worked that sweet, hard nipple, rolling his tongue around it, teasing it with his teeth—and sliding a hand around to the back of her at the same time, working the clasp of the bra until it gave.

He went on, kissing one breast and then the other, as he guided the satin straps down her shoulders. She straightened her arms for him, her body a bow, surging up to his mouth as he suckled on her.

The bra fell away. He lifted his head again and she opened her eyes, glazed now. So hungry.

As hungry as he was...

"Get rid of this, all of it...." His voice was gruffer than he meant it to be as he felt behind her for the hook and the zipper at the back of her skinny little skirt. She let out a small cry—and then she helped him, pushing his hands out of the way, unzipping it herself.

He shoved it over the singing curve of her hips, going on down with it, dropping to his knees before her, grabbing her pantyhose and the lacy red triangle that covered her sex from him and dragging them down. She teetered a little, but then rested her hands on his shoulders to kick off those pointy red shoes. Once the shoes were gone, he took her by the waist and sat her back on the end of the bed.

The panties and stockings were bunched just below her knees. He got them the rest of the way down, pulled them off the ends of her red-tipped toes and tossed the wad of nylon and silk over his shoulder.

She cried his name.

He glanced up at her, liking the sound of it, his name, so needful on her sweet plump mouth, which was bruised now, fuller than ever from his kisses.

"Lie down," he whispered.

With a tiny, hungry moan, she dropped back onto the bed.

He took her knees and eased them over his shoulders and he moved in, close. A long shiver coursed through her. He put his hand on her, on her white belly, which tightened in response to his touch. She lifted her head off the bed and looked down at him, that newly red hair falling along the wonderful pink curve of her cheek.

"Aaron…"

He touched the shining brown curls at the place where her thighs met.

She gasped. And she let her head fall back.

Gently, he parted her. She was moaning by then, pressing herself eagerly to his seeking mouth.

He tasted her, that most private part of her. It was slick and soft, ready for him. He ran his tongue along the secret folds, moving in all the closer, tasting her more deeply, pressing a palm on her belly, to hold her in place.

Her hips moved, slowly at first, hesitantly. Then faster, and faster, her body bowing up off the white quilt, her sex opening wider, inviting his tongue.

He accepted her invitation, deepening the forbidden kiss, loving the taste of her, the way she cried out, the way she pressed closer, ever closer, her body reaching, striving—seeking the soft explosion of fulfillment.

It came at last. With a wild cry, she went rigid. He drank in the tender pulsing that signaled her completion.

He stayed with her through the pulsing, until she went lax and easy, sinking into the bed with a final long sigh. Then, very gently, he eased out from under the sweet weight of her thighs. He moved up onto the bed with her, turning on his side away from her, as he reached for a condom from the three on the night table.

He had it on in seconds.

He felt her soft hand, touching his back, stroking. He rolled to face her. She stared at him, mouth soft, eyes glazed.

He went into her waiting arms.

Celia cried out when he entered her—a cry of wonder, of excitement, of pure physical joy.

Oh, it felt so good. So right, to have him inside her. He stayed up on his elbows and he looked down at her, watching her.

She stared right back at him, all her earlier fears

and anxiousness seared away by his kisses, by his wonderful, slow, delicious caresses. He moved smoothly, surely, settling deeply into her. She accepted him, her body opening willingly to accommodate him.

She thought, *I love you, Aaron. I do. I love you so....*

But she didn't say the words. She knew he didn't want the words. So she was careful, so careful, not to say them out loud.

He thrust in harder. She took him. She could take anything, all he could give. She wrapped her legs around him, pulling him closer, taking him deeper.

He closed his eyes first. His bronze lashes swept down and his head went back, straining, the tendons standing out on his powerful neck.

She watched him, her love a searing flame within her, as the slow, deep rhythm of their lovemaking intensified. He surged into her, faster. She went right with him, her body rising, the pleasure expanding, every nerve singing.

And it happened. He hit the peak on a final, hard, deep thrust. She felt that—felt him contracting in spasms within her.

And then, she was lost, too, her body shimmering, all of her shattering into a thousand bright shards. Behind her eyes, the world was a million points of glittering light cascading within a hot and velvety darkness. And she was inside it, a part of that wonderful light-scattered darkness, falling forever into eternity, through a magical night of a billion stars.

Chapter Twelve

Aaron's lady.

Celia heard them whispering. She knew what they called her.

She smiled when she heard it. Because she was proud that it was so.

It took a little over a week of the two of them together in this wholly new way before word got around. They were discreet—during business hours, anyway. But they lived where they worked. And sometimes, when Aaron would take her to dinner at the Placer Room or Casa D'Oro, well, they couldn't help the way they looked at each other, couldn't prevent the occasional tender caress.

They were surrounded, after all, by interested observers. By maids and floor supervisors, managers and waitresses, vice presidents and security personnel. Everyone at High Sierra made it their business to know what was going on with the boss. It was, after all, to their advantage to know.

They had known about Jennifer. And they had known about the dazzling string of beautiful women before her.

And it was inevitable that they would come to know about Celia.

They treated her with respect and a sort of tenderness, a protectiveness, that warmed her. Not that they hadn't all respected her before, when she was strictly Aaron's secretary and personal assistant.

But now, it was...different, the way they looked at her, the way they deferred to her, the way the chefs and waiters in High Sierra's restaurants would fuss over her, the way all the bartenders suddenly knew that the Cosmopolitan was her drink of choice.

Aaron's lady, after all, helped to keep Aaron happy. And that was good for everyone.

A few days after Celia and Aaron first made love, Jane called and demanded to know what was going on.

So Celia told her. And Jane said, "Well. Are you happy?"

"You know, it's like a dream..."

Jane made a small, irritated noise in her throat. "Stop evading. It's a yes-or-no question."

"Okay. I'm happy." And she was. She truly was.

"But you want more."

"I didn't say that."

"So...you *don't* want more?"

"The hard fact is, I'm not going to get more. And so I think it would be a good idea to be happy with what I've got."

"Snippy, snippy."

"Sorry. I didn't mean to be."

"Hey," said Jane softly. "Enjoy yourself. Okay?"

"I will, Janey. I *am.*"

Jillian called about fifteen minutes after Celia said goodbye to Jane. "I hear that you and Aaron are an item. And that you're loving it."

"That's right. I am."

"Good for you, Ceil. Still like your hair?"

"I love it."

"Does Aaron like it?"

"*He* loves it."

"I'm sorry. I've got to ask. What were you wearing, the first time he—"

"That cinnamon-red suit we picked out at—"

Jillian let out a moan of pure pleasure. "Oh, I knew it. You're a dream in that suit. I'm so pleased with myself."

Celia couldn't help smiling. "Jilly, I'm crazy about everything you did for me. You've come a long way from dyeing Jane's hair green."

"I have, haven't I—and what next, between you and Aaron?"

"I intend to enjoy myself, to savor every minute with him, for as long as it lasts."

"Guess what? That was going to be my advice, exactly. Have a great time."

"I will."

* * *

It was no hardship, savoring every minute with Aaron. He treated her like a queen, made love to her as if he couldn't get enough of her. And he showered her with jewels—an emerald bracelet, a platinum lariat necklace, a string of absolutely perfect ten-millimeter Mikimoto pearls. At first, she wondered if he had another assistant stashed somewhere, someone he wasn't sleeping with, someone he could instruct to go out and find charming, pricey trinkets for his latest lady.

But Celia did keep all of his personal accounts. And she figured out soon enough how he came by the gifts. He was bidding for them on the Internet.

That discovery pleased her—first of all, because *he* was choosing the gifts himself, thinking of her when he did it, looking for things he thought she might like. And also, well, it was just so *like* him to find gifts that way, now that his secretary was the person he was buying the gifts for. He could check in at the auction site periodically, see what else was available, raise a bid if he needed to—and all without leaving his desk.

Oh, it was a wonderful time, really, full of memories to treasure. They spent the days working together—and the nights wrapped up in each other's arms.

Two weeks went by in the blink of an eye.

Then, the first Monday in April, Caitlin dropped in unannounced.

Aaron's mother breezed into the office at eleven in the morning, wearing black velvet jeans, skin-tight, of course. For a woman in her fifties, Caitlin certainly was fit. Her shirt was Western-cut, as always—black, with lots of glittery yellow fringe.

Caitlin sashayed in and swung a leg up on the edge of Celia's desk. "Hello, baby doll."

"Hi, Caitlin. What a surprise."

"Where's my son?"

"Aaron isn't in right this minute, but—"

"Well, good. I didn't come to see him, anyway."

"Oh?"

"Thanks for doing my taxes. It's a major load off my mind."

"You're welcome." Celia knew what was coming. And it was.

"Now. Down to what matters."

"Yes?"

"Word gets around. The gaming industry's a small one in a lot of ways."

"Oh?"

Caitlin chuckled that sexy deep chuckle of hers. "Sweetie, you should see your pretty little face. Oh, yes. Waitin' for the other shoe to drop, as they say— and you're lookin' good, by the way. I like your hair. And you've changed your makeup, haven't you?"

"As a matter of fact—"

Caitlin beat the air with a hand—a signal that she didn't need to hear more. "Well, like I said. It looks good. And I might as well save the effort at subtlety. We all know I'm not. I'll just say it out straight. I heard about you and Aaron. That looks good to me, too—then again, you knew it would, since I told you so last month. What I want to know is, when's the weddin'?"

The wedding? Where had that come from?

Celia had expected Caitlin to find out about her new relationship with Aaron. And, judging by the things Caitlin had said to her three weeks ago, she'd been pretty sure that Aaron's mother would approve. But *marriage?* Surely Caitlin had to know enough about her own son to realize a wedding wasn't part of the equation.

"My sweet darlin', you look like someone just shot your dog."

Celia thought, at that moment, of Jane. Jane would tell her to be up-front and direct about this. And really, that was probably the best way to go. "Caitlin, you have to know that your oldest son is not the marrying kind."

Caitlin beat the air with her hand again, as if fending off Celia's words. "Sure he is. He just doesn't know it yet."

"No. Seriously, he's a very bright man and he knows how he feels."

"No. He doesn't. He knows what he *thinks* he feels. It's not the same thing. He needs to get what's good for him, whether he likes it or not."

"Caitlin, listen to yourself. Don't you remember what you told me a few weeks ago? How you were staying out of this, one hundred percent?"

"Well, sure. But you worry me a little. Sometimes I think maybe you haven't got the stomach for what needs to be done. And I can't help being me, and being me means not fooling around. I want to see some action, you know?"

"I swear, you have no shame."

Caitlin didn't even flinch. "That's right, I don't. I go after what I want when I want it, and I don't let anything stand in my way."

"Well, that's great. That's terrific. But this isn't about you, it's about Aaron. And me. And we'd like to run our own lives, if you don't mind."

Caitlin leaned forward. "Baby doll, I do mind, if you're gonna make a mess of things."

More than a little overwhelmed by all the glittery fringe and musky perfume, Celia leaned back. "It's just…"

"What?"

"Caitlin, this is not your business."

"Sure it is. He's my son and I want him to get what's best for him."

"That's for him to decide—and come on. You never settled down yourself. Why would you think your son would want to?"

"I'd like to think he's smarter than me. And besides, he's a man. A man needs a good woman. A man needs…a home base."

"Well, I'm flattered, sincerely, that you think I'm the right woman for Aaron on a permanent basis, but—"

The phone jangled to life. "Excuse me." Celia reached for it.

Caitlin slammed a hand down on the receiver. "Uh-uh. Leave it."

Celia sighed. "Caitlin. Let go of the phone."

"You've got voice mail. Get a little use out of it."

"This is so overbearing of you."

Caitlin just stared at her, black eyes gleaming. The

phone rang four times. When it was finally silent, Caitlin folded her arms over her impressive breasts. "You love him, right?"

"It's none of your business."

"I'll take that as a yes. So. You love him, you want what's best for him. Right?"

"As I said before, what's best for Aaron is for Aaron to decide."

Caitlin threw back her head and groaned aloud. "Listen. You marrying my boy will be the best thing that ever happened to him. You'll be doing him the biggest favor you ever did for anyone. And since you love him, it's natural you'd want to do right by him."

"He does not want to get married."

"I want you to get a ring on your finger."

"Well, as I've said a number of times now, what you want is not what matters here."

"Do whatever you have to do."

"I can't believe you're saying this."

"A baby would be nice…"

"Oh, Caitlin. That is so unacceptable."

"He'll thank you for it later."

"No, he won't. What are you thinking? He's not going to thank me for *tricking* him."

"Sure he will. Eventually."

"Caitlin. Whoa. Stop. Hold on."

Caitlin sat back a little. "What?"

"I am not going to manipulate Aaron into marrying me. It's wrong. And I won't do it. He doesn't want to get married. Ever. He's made that very clear."

Caitlin made a humphing sound. "Well, if you believe that, then what are you doing with him?"

"I beg your pardon?"

"Oh, don't go gettin' all huffy on me. You know what I'm sayin'. We both know that you *are* the marrying kind. You're a nice girl who wants a husband, like all nice girls do."

"That is *so* not fair."

"What's *fair* got to do with it? What's *fair* got to do with any damn thing? Haven't you heard, darlin'? Life is *not* fair."

"Fine. All right. You may have a point there. But that crack about nice girls...for your information, Caitlin, there are nice girls in this world who have more on their minds than getting a ring on their finger."

"Well, you could be right. Maybe there are nice girls like that. But you're not one of them, not when it comes to Aaron, and we both know it. One thing you learn in my business, it's how to read a face. And I can read yours, baby doll, every time you look in my son's direction—every time someone mentions his name. So don't tell me lies. You know you're no good at them. Don't you sit there and try to convince me you don't want to marry my darlin' boy."

"I didn't say that."

Caitlin tossed that hard black head of hair. "Hah."

"What I said was, *he* doesn't want to marry *me*."

"And I said, he *does*. He just doesn't know it yet."

"Caitlin, this conversation is going in circles."

"You're right." Caitlin swung her leg off the desk and stood, sucking in her stomach and poking out those big, proud breasts. She smoothed her velvet jeans—as if they could possibly have gotten wrinkled, tight as they were. "I'm goin' downstairs to have a look around the place, see how things are doing.'' She clicked her tongue. ''Drives Aaron crazy, when I do that—will he be back around here soon?''

''After lunch.''

''Hmm. You know what?''

''Caitlin, I don't like the look in your eye.''

Aaron's mother had the nerve to flutter her fake black eyelashes. ''I don't think I'll stick around.''

''But—''

''Let me speak. I want you to give a little thought to the things I've said to you.''

''Caitlin—''

''I'm not done. Give what I said some thought. And remember, if there's anything—*anything*—I can do to help you out with this, you just let me know. As for right now, I'm goin' down to the casino, gonna walk the floor a little, just enough so word will get back to Aaron that I'm as irritating as ever—gotta keep him guessin', after all.''

''No, you don't.''

''Sure, I do, sweetie pie. Aaron wouldn't know how to handle it if all of a sudden, I turned *reasonable* on him.''

''How do you know he couldn't handle it? Have you ever tried being reasonable?''

''No, and I don't believe I'll start now. What I *will* do is walk the floor a little, then head for the airport and catch a flight home.'' Celia knew there was a clincher coming. And there was. ''I'll let *you* tell him the real reason I came. That is, if you *want* to tell him. Because, baby doll, I promise you, he'll never hear it from me.''

* * *

Celia intended to tell him. She honestly did.

He returned to the office at two-thirty. One of his managers had already reported that his mother had been down on the casino floor. "Is she here?" he asked grimly, shooting a put-upon look at the shut door to his own office.

"No. But she was—at a little after eleven. When she left, she told me she was going down to the casino for a while and then she was going back to the airport to catch a plane for home."

He was scowling. "I don't get it. What did she want?"

Celia recognized the moment for just what it was: time to come clean.

But when she opened her mouth, evasions came out. "Well, she thanked me. For doing her taxes."

"That's all? She flew down here just to thank you for doing her taxes?"

Celia shrugged, letting him read whatever he chose to in the cryptic gesture.

He said, "I do not understand that woman. Never have, never will."

"I'd have to say, you're not alone."

He hitched a leg up on the desk—as his mother had done a few hours before. "Well. She's gone now. I think I'll just be grateful for small favors."

"Good idea."

He leaned toward her. Her midsection heated and her breath caught.

Just before his lips met hers, she made herself sit back. "Uh-uh. Not in the office."

"Celia."

"Yes, Aaron?"

"Admit it." His voice, pitched low for her ears alone, caused a long, delicious shiver to slip along the surface of her skin.

"Admit what?"

"You want me to kiss you."

"Oh, yes. I do."

He leaned forward again.

She put up a hand, between his lips and hers. "But not in the office."

He lifted an eyebrow. "Such admirable restraint." He stood. "Tonight." The word was a promise.

She nodded, slowly. "Yes. Please. Tonight."

She was thinking, I *will* tell him. Later. I honestly will.

He was coming to her rooms at eight. When he got there, she would pour him a drink and sit him down and tell him everything, all of it—from Caitlin's remarks in New Venice three weeks before, to everything she'd said that morning.

But every time Celia imagined herself doing that, she found herself wincing and squirming in her chair.

It was just too…embarrassing to go into it. No matter how she tried to put the words together in her mind, it made her feel *less* somehow, to tell him the truth about this. Because deep in her heart, she wanted exactly what Caitlin had said she wanted: to marry the man she loved.

But she had no illusions. She honestly didn't. They had a clear understanding on the subject of marriage. There wasn't going to be one.

And she didn't want to go into it. She didn't *need*

to go into it. There was no point in going into it. She was a strong woman and she knew where she stood with him, that what they had wouldn't last forever.

But while it did last, damn it, she had a right to her pride.

Let Caitlin play her absurd matchmaking games. Celia had made herself clear to Aaron's mother. She was not, in any way, going along with the older woman's schemes.

And she was not going to report to Aaron the ridiculous things his mother had said.

Let Caitlin do it herself—or not. It was nothing to Celia. She was not saying a word.

The first thing she did when he came to her door was to wrap her arms around his neck. "Welcome."

He held her lightly, grinning down at her. "I think, maybe, you're glad to see me."

Shamelessly, she rubbed her hips against him. "Um. I *know* you're glad to see me...."

His wonderful hands slid down her back and over the twin curves of her bottom. He cupped her, pulled her up snug and close, so she could feel even more intimately how much he wanted her. "I suppose you've got dinner waiting...."

"No. I thought you could use a little time to relax first. I asked them to send it up at about nine."

"An hour."

"Um-hm."

They kissed, a deep, seeking kiss, right there, in her entryway, with the door to the hall standing wide open so anyone who walked by might have seen them.

Neither of them cared about that. Why should they? Everyone knew they were lovers and they were on their own time, in her private space.

When he finally lifted his head, her whole body was humming. He scooped her up into his arms, kicked the door shut, and headed for her bedroom.

They went to Atlantic City that weekend, to look over a small casino/hotel Silver Standard was acquiring. Celia stayed by Aaron's side, doing her job, tending to the details, keeping things running smoothly.

And when they were alone, she went into his arms.

Saturday night, in bed in their hotel suite, he asked her when she'd be going on the pill. They had talked about it earlier, and she'd told him that she would.

She traced the line of his jaw with a lazy finger. "Well, I've been to my doctor...."

"And?"

She stroked his hair, lightly, at the temple. "I got a prescription. I also had it filled...."

"And?"

She kissed the cleft in his chin. "Now I have to wait until the Sunday after my next period to start taking them."

"And that will be?"

She thought for a moment, realized her period was due in the next few days. "Soon," she said. "Very soon..." He wrapped his arms around her and put his mouth on hers and for a while, she forgot everything but the magic of his kiss.

But their conversation had reminded her that her

period was due. She waited for the signs, for the bloated feeling and the cramping.

The signs didn't come.

By Friday, it seemed as if she thought of nothing else but the fact that she was late—and what that might mean.

On Saturday, she left High Sierra and went to a drugstore downtown, where she bought a home test. The instructions on the box said the test could determine pregnancy the day after a missed period. Back in her rooms, Celia went straight to the bathroom off her bedroom. She sat on the edge of the tub and opened the box.

Inside, along with the necessary equipment, she found a lengthy brochure containing detailed instructions, including the information that taking the test first thing in the morning minimized the possibility of getting a false negative result.

Carefully, Celia folded the brochure back into a tidy square and returned it to the box. She put the box in the cabinet under the sink.

Tomorrow morning, she thought. Tomorrow, I'll know.

That night, she and Aaron had dinner in the Placer Room, where the tablecloths were snowy white and the booths were half-moon-shaped, upholstered in glove-soft black leather. The walls were papered in stamped antique-gold foil. Aaron ordered a nice bottle of pinot grigio. After Aaron tasted it and nodded, the wine steward filled Celia's glass.

She looked at that full glass and knew she would

not touch it. That was the moment she understood her own intention. If the test tomorrow came out positive, she was going to keep the baby.

Oh, God. What would Aaron think about that?

She wasn't sure she wanted to know.

Aaron's estranged cousin, Jonas Bravo, the man they called the Bravo Billionaire, also had dinner in the Placer Room that night. He and his platinum-haired wife, Emma, sat three booths down from Celia and Aaron.

Aaron never so much as glanced their way, which didn't surprise Celia in the least. Caitlin and her brood had always lived as if the other Bravos didn't exist. After all, Aaron's father, Blake, had been disinherited and completely cut off from the rest of the family by the time he met Caitlin. And then, before her youngest, Cade, was even born, Blake Bravo had faked his own death and vanished. He took a second wife and fathered another son. But before that, he'd kidnapped his own nephew for revenge against the family that had scorned him.

In the end, thirty years later, Jonas Bravo got his brother back, and the evil Blake was truly gone— according to the newspapers, he'd died last May of heart failure in an Oklahoma Hospital.

New Venice had been abuzz with gossip as the story unfolded. A lot of folks had assumed that the branches of the family would reunite at last.

But it hadn't happened. For the Nevada Bravos, things stayed as they had always been. Caitlin and her sons continued to behave as though they were the only Bravos in the world. Which meant that Jonas and his lovely wife could eat dinner three booths down from Aaron and Celia and not so much as a nod of recognition would pass between the two men.

Emma Bravo, however, was another story. More than once, she caught Celia's eye. Each time she did, a big, friendly smile would spread across her pretty face. That smile was contagious. Celia couldn't help but smile back.

Aaron noticed the exchange of looks between the women. He said, very softly, "Celia, what are you up to?"

She felt angry with him, suddenly—mostly, she knew, from sheer nerves over what she'd learn tomorrow when she finally took that test. "Nothing. Just smiling at someone who smiled at me. Is that all right with you?"

He frowned at her. "What's the matter?"

She thought, *I'm terrified I might be pregnant.* She said, "Well, don't you think it's about time you and your cousin stopped ignoring each other? I mean, I understand, your mother is a proud woman. And she was loyal to your father's memory and refused to have anything to do with the family who cut him off. But now the truth has come out about Blake, don't you think everyone should forgive and forget?"

He picked up his wineglass and sipped, then set the glass down. "Celia." He spoke quietly, thoughtfully. "I have nothing at all against Jonas Bravo, or any other Bravo, for that matter. Yes, my mother used to say she hated them, back when Cade and Will and I were kids. But you know Caitlin, a drama queen if there ever was one. She never mentions them at all these days. We're all going along just fine. There's no animosity.''

''And no connection, either.''

''Why does there need to be a connection?''

''Well, because you are *family* to each other.''

He shook his head. ''I know who my family is. My crazy mother and my two brothers. That's about all the family I can handle, believe me.''

''But—''

''Celia.'' He caught her hand, kissed the back of it. ''Stop.'' He gestured at her full plate. ''Are you going to eat? You've hardly touched your food—or your wine.''

Gently, she pulled her hand free of his. She picked up her fork and her steak knife and went to work on her filet mignon. His phone must have vibrated, because he murmured, ''Excuse me.''

''Of course.''

He took the phone out and answered, first glancing at the display. ''Tony, what is it?''

Tony Jarvis, she supposed, with some question or other that couldn't wait till later. ''Yes,'' he said. ''All right... That's fine. Go ahead.''

Celia ate her dinner and promised herself she wouldn't bring up the subject of Jonas Bravo again. Aaron's relationship with his cousin was Aaron's business. She was on edge about the test tomorrow, and a contrary part of her was looking for any excuse to start an argument.

But really, she didn't want to argue with Aaron. She loved him and she intended to treasure every moment she had with him.

When he slipped his phone back into his pocket, she leaned toward him, till her shoulder brushed his arm. "Sorry…"

He put his hand on her knee beneath the tablecloth and gave it a tender squeeze.

Later, when they got to her place, Aaron asked again if something was bothering her.

She lied some more. "No. Why?"

"I don't know. On and off, all night, you've seemed…far away. Distracted."

She shut the door and engaged the lock. Then she turned into his arms and slid her hands around his neck. "Bring me back to the here-and-now."

His glance tracked from her mouth to her eyes and back to her mouth again. "This does look promising."

"Kiss me."

"You're sure a kiss will do it?"

"I think we really ought to give it a try."

"Like this?" His mouth came down on hers.

"Oh, yes…" She breathed the words against his parted lips.

He lifted his head. "More?"

"Please."

So he slanted his mouth the other way and claimed her lips again.

Oh, sweet heaven, the man did know how to kiss. He started undressing her, right there in her small entryway. She was naked in no time, at which point he began guiding her backward, toward the living room, leaving her little black slip dress, strapless black bra and panties, as well as her spike-heeled satin shoes in a mound on the floor of the foyer.

She'd thought they were headed for her bedroom. But he detoured to the living-room sofa. He pulled her over there and sat down and pulled her on top of him, so she sat astride his lean hips. Shameless, she rubbed herself against him, moaning at the feel of him, that ridge of hardness and heat beneath the zipper of his slacks.

She went to work on his jacket, getting it off, tossing it away, kissing him deeply as she worked at his tie.

"Can't wait..." he groaned against her mouth. He started working at his belt buckle.

She realized she was in the way. With a groan, she slid off him. They fumbled together at his belt. Once it was undone, she grabbed the end of it and slithered it free of the belt loops, tossing it to the floor. He unzipped his slacks. She pulled the elastic of his boxers out of the way, freeing him. Oh, he was so beautiful. So silky and big and hot...

She felt his warm breath against her ear. "Ride me..."

Moaning in pure delight, she slid one bare leg over him. Oh yes. She felt him, there, nudging the feminine heart of her. She was wet and open. So ready....

She lowered her body onto—

At the last possible second, she realized the huge mistake she was about to make.

She scrambled off him.

He swore. "What the—"

"Wait right there."

He groaned—and then he swore again. "Celia. What's going on?"

"You know. Protection."

He blinked. "Oh, God. Right."

They stared at each other.

It *had* happened before. The only difference between now and then was that tonight, she'd remembered in time to correct the mistake.

Worry jabbed at her again. Maybe it didn't matter at this point. Maybe tomorrow, she'd discover it was too late, anyway.

She pushed the worry to the back of her mind. It would still be there tomorrow.

And for now, well, better to proceed in a responsible manner.

He looked down at the evidence of his desire for her, pointing boldly north. Then he lifted his gaze to hers. "Where do you think you're going?"

"To get the—"

"Stop right there." He reached in his pocket and pulled out a foil-wrapped pouch. "Is this what you're looking for?"

A giggle of pure surprise escaped her. "Where did you get that?"

He grinned. "I've decided it's best to be ready at all times, in all circumstances."

"Ah." She looked at him, loving him—and wanting him so. It was going to be all right, she just knew it. Everything was going to work out fine. And for now, well, she couldn't resist the promise in those blue, blue eyes. She didn't *want* to resist.

Softly, she whispered, "Good thinking."

He was already rolling the condom down over himself. "Get back here," he growled. Then he looked up at her, eyes so tender. "Please."

She climbed into his lap again. He whispered her name on a pleasured sigh, as she slid down onto the waiting length of him. Oh, it felt so good to be joined with him. It felt so right, so very fine....

He lifted her slightly, gathering her to him, first licking a circle around her left breast, then capturing it, tenderly drawing the nipple to a hard, aching bead. Celia felt the silken cord of arousal, that connection between her breast and her womb, shimmering, tightening, quivering like a drawn bow.

She let her head fall back and moaned low in her throat, riding him slow, in long, wet, lovely strokes. "So good..." she whispered.

He made a low noise that sounded very much like agreement.

And then he encircled her waist with his lean hands, pressing her down as he slid up harder into her, increasing the hungry, rolling rhythm.

Everything flew away.

She cried out.

He took her mouth, kissing her as fulfillment sang through her, a burning melody, fire-bright.

He got up to go at a little after two. She walked him to the door.

"Tomorrow," he said. "Lunch?"

"Yes."

"I'll call, around ten..."

"Okay."

He gathered her into his arms and kissed her good-night.

Oh, the man could kiss. Her midsection was melting, her knees turning boneless.

A kiss like his should never end.

But it did. He left her. She returned to her bed.

She felt drowsy, at first, soothed and satisfied by their lovemaking. She anticipated a few hours of restful sleep.

But the drowsiness passed. Sleep never came. She waited, wide awake, until five. And then she got up and went to the bathroom and took the test.

It was positive.

And as she looked at the double pink line in the result window, it almost seemed that she could hear Caitlin Bravo's low, knowing laughter echoing in her ears.

Chapter Thirteen

Was she surprised?

No, she decided. Not really.

She felt kind of numb, actually. Numb, but calm.

And determined.

She did know one thing for certain right at that moment. She was keeping this baby.

Gee. Wouldn't Aaron be thrilled?

She recalled how he'd asked if she was pregnant all those weeks ago, when she'd first confessed her love to him.

Maybe that was how she'd break it to him.

Guess what, Aaron? I wasn't pregnant then. But I am now....

She tossed the test wand into the wastebasket and went back to her bedroom, where she dropped to the side of her tangled bed and looked down at her bare red-tipped toes.

She sat that way for perhaps five minutes, gathering her red robe close around her, hugging herself tight, thinking that she ought to *do* something—but not sure exactly what.

Maybe what she needed was a little good advice.

She reached for the phone, punched the auto-dial button for Jane—and then disconnected the call before it went through. What was Jane going to tell her?

The usual.

Honesty is the way to go here. Tell him the truth.

And surprise, surprise. Jane would be right.

But she didn't need Jane to rub it in, thank you very much. She knew she would have to tell Aaron that she was having his baby. What she didn't know was how she was going to make herself do it.

And how she would bear his reaction. That was another thing she didn't want to think about.

Really, she'd rather talk to Jilly than Jane right at the moment. Celia loved Jane dearly, but Jane was always so firm and uncompromising when it came to the tough questions in life. Jilly would be more easygoing, less judgmental—on this subject, anyway. Jilly was always more interested in those she loved getting what they really wanted, not so much of a stickler on truth and integrity.

Celia punched the button for her other best friend—and then cut it off in mid-dial as well. What advice would Jilly have for her? What to *wear* when she told him?

No. Jillian wouldn't have the answers here.

And besides, Celia didn't *need* answers. She knew what to do. She just utterly dreaded the thought of doing it.

She stared at the phone in her hand—and experienced a powerful impulse to call Caitlin, to scream rude, incoherent, hopeless things at her. And then to slam the phone down before Caitlin could say anything back.

Celia waited, clutching the phone, as that dangerous urge slowly faded away. When it was gone, she felt like a balloon with all the air let out of it—drained and limp.

Very gently, she hung up.

Then she took off her robe and got under the covers. She turned on her side and she drew her legs up close to her body and wrapped both arms around her knees.

All tucked into herself, seeking a comfort she didn't really expect to find, she closed her eyes.

The ringing of the phone jangled her awake.

"Huh?" Her eyes popped open. She was looking straight at her bedside clock. It was 10:02.

The phone went on ringing. Celia lay perfectly still, staring at the clock. After four rings, she heard the machine in the other room pick up the call. She watched the clock and saw the time change. 10:03. She closed her eyes and went back to sleep.

The next time the phone rang, she didn't even open her eyes. She rolled to her other side and wrapped the pillow over her head. She drifted off again.

The phone rang for the third time not long after the

second. With a groan, Celia turned over. The clock was waiting. Ten past twelve. Not even morning anymore.

She dragged herself to a sitting position and grabbed the receiver in mid-ring. "Hello," she grumbled into the mouthpiece.

"There you are." It broke her heart, just hearing his voice. "Still in bed?"

"'Fraid so." She gripped the phone much tighter than she needed to and told herself she was not going to burst into self-pitying tears.

"I called twice before. No answer."

"I confess. I was sleeping."

"Well, it's time you got up."

"Yes. Yes, I guess it is."

"How about if we—"

She cut him off. "Aaron."

A pause, then he asked, "What?"

"Do you think you could come here, to my rooms, in say, half an hour? There's something I have to tell you."

"Celia—"

"No. Really. I do need to talk with you. And I need to do it face-to-face."

He was quiet again. It was far from a comfortable silence.

"Aaron? Did you hear me?"

"Of course, I heard you."

"Will you—"

He cut her off. "I'll be there. Thirty minutes."

The line went dead.

Celia yanked the phone away from her ear and stared at it, unable to believe what she had just done.

What was the matter with her? She was maybe three weeks pregnant, tops. She'd only taken the test a few hours ago.

Yes, she did have to tell him. Sooner or later.

But right *now,* today?

Even Jane wouldn't have expected *that* of her.

With a groan of pure misery, Celia shook the phone at the far wall. The silly display of frustration did nothing to change the fact that in the next half hour Aaron would be knocking on her door, expecting to hear what she just had to tell him immediately.

She slammed the phone back in its cradle.

And then she flopped back on the bed. "*Why* did I do that? Why, why, why?" she asked of no one in particular.

Not surprisingly, she got no answer.

Aaron arrived at Celia's door twenty-eight minutes from the time he'd hung up the phone. He punched the buzzer.

The door swung back immediately, leading him to believe she'd been waiting right behind it. She wore flared black slacks and a red sweater. No makeup. Her face had that scrubbed-clean, innocent look. She smelled dewy and sweet. Fresh from the shower.

Conflicting urges tore at him.

He wanted to grab her and hold her and kiss that soft, plump mouth.

He also wanted to demand to know what the hell was going on. He'd sensed something wasn't right for a few days now. Last night, he'd even asked her—more than once, too—what was bothering her. She'd said there was nothing.

But looking in her troubled face right now, he knew for certain that she had lied.

And he was angry.

And strangely fearful, as well.

He didn't understand his own emotions in this. He only knew that little Celia Tuttle mattered to him in ways no other woman ever had. They worked together and they played together. They shared a bed almost every night. He spent more time with her than he ever had with any of the other women he'd been involved with romantically.

He kept waiting to get bored.

But it wasn't happening.

In fact, he seemed to be moving in the opposite direction. The more time he spent with her, the more he *wanted* to spend with her. She'd become very important to him.

Too important, probably.

"Please come in," she said, way too formally, reminding him of the first time he'd been here, to her rooms—that day in early March, when she'd confessed that she loved him.

They went to the living room. He took an easy chair and she sat on the couch.

She folded her hands and looked down at them.

What? he was thinking. *Talk. Tell me what the hell is going on.*

But he kept his mouth shut. The way he saw it,

she'd asked him to come here, said she had to talk
to him.

So all right. Let her say whatever she had to say
without any coaxing from him.

Celia knew very well that the ball was in her court.

She'd gotten him here and it was her job now to
tell him why. She cleared her throat. "Um, well, I..."
and the words kind of petered out. She stared at her
folded hands. She didn't want to look up. She didn't
want to meet his eyes.

She didn't want to tell him what she knew she *had*
to tell him.

And as she sat there, in that awful, yawning silence,
it occurred to her that she...couldn't.

She could not tell him. Not right now, not today.

She'd barely learned the truth herself. The baby—
their baby—wouldn't be born for months and months.

Of course, Aaron would have to know eventually.

But he certainly didn't need to get the news this
minute.

Didn't she have a right to a little time for herself?
A little breather, where she could begin to deal with
the enormity of what was happening in her life?

In the back of her mind somewhere, she could hear
Jane chiding, *Tell him. He has a right to know. He's
the baby's father. And honesty is always the best policy....*

Oh, shut up, Jane, she thought.

But that one word, *honesty* seemed to echo in her
brain. Oh, yes. There *was* a central problem here—
beyond the fact that they'd messed up a few times
and forgotten to practice safe and protected sex. That

central problem was all about a lack of honesty. On her part.

Which was ironic, since she had told herself she was being so straightforward, so up-front, so *truthful* in this love affair.

But the whole time, she'd been lying—lying to *herself.* She was exactly what Caitlin had accused her of being. A nice girl who wanted a good man to marry her.

Correction. A nice, *pregnant* girl. A pregnant girl who wanted her baby's father to marry her.

She looked up. He was waiting, jaw set, eyes watchful. He was on to her now. He knew for certain there was a serious problem of some kind. At this point, he wouldn't buy her denials for a minute, should she try to resurrect them. If she sent him away now without telling him about the baby, it would do serious damage to his opinion of her.

And she valued that, his high regard. Maybe he didn't love her, didn't feel the same searing joy and agonizing pain at the thought of her, at the very mention of her name, as she did when it came to him. But he did respect her. He *liked* her.

And she never wanted to lose that—his good opinion of her as a person—not if she could help it, anyway.

He kept on watching her, waiting for her to come out with it.

She stared back at him, into his eyes. As they regarded each other, it seemed to Celia that all her excuses and evasions, all her cowardly hopes for putting off this conversation, softened to formlessness and melted away.

She understood. There really was no backing out now. She had to do it, had to say it, now, today. She had called him here and sat him down and he had a right to hear the truth from her lips. He needed to know what was happening, and to know it now.

It was, after all, his baby, too. She couldn't turn back time, couldn't do the past over. She'd been careless and she was pregnant and the best she could hope for was to handle the situation with dignity and frankness.

She yanked her shoulders back and aimed her chin high. "Aaron," she said. "I'm pregnant."

He didn't move. He didn't speak—for a hideous count of ten. Then he opened his jacket, took his phone from the inside pocket and tossed it on the wheat-colored Berber that covered the floor. It took her a second or two to realize it must have been vibrating with an incoming call.

She said, "Please. If it's important, you can go ahead and—"

"Celia."

"Hmm?"

"Forget the damn phone call."

She gulped, nodded. "Okay."

"When did you find out?"

"This morning. I took a home test. The results were positive."

He tipped his head to the side, thinking. Then he asked, "How dependable is a test like that?"

"Very. They're accurate the day after a missed period. I'm four days late."

He was quiet again. Then he muttered, "Last night." His eyes accused her. "I kept asking you what was the matter."

"Yes, I know."

"But you said there was nothing."

"I lied."

"Why?"

"Because I wanted to take the test first. It could have been a false alarm. I didn't see any reason for both of us to worry."

He considered her words. After a minute, he nodded. "All right. That makes sense."

She realized she'd been holding her breath. She let it out, slowly.

He asked, "Now what?"

She told him the next thing he needed to know. "I'm going to keep this baby."

That got her one of his wry half smiles. "Why doesn't that surprise me?"

She forged on. "I'll raise the baby alone, if I have to. But I'd rather not. I believe that, if possible, a baby should have *both* of his—or her—parents."

"Ah," he said. "I see."

"You disagree?"

He lifted one shoulder, sketching a shrug. "Well, I'd have to say, that is the conventional wisdom. But what would I know about it? I was raised in a bar by a woman who never did manage to settle on one man."

"Aaron?"

"What?"

"I think you know where I'm going with this."

"Let's say I have a pretty good idea."

"Well, I guess I'll just ask you."

"Go for it."

"Aaron, will you marry me?"

"Yes, Celia. I will."

Chapter Fourteen

Yes.

He'd said yes.

Celia stood up. Then she felt a little dizzy. So she sat down again.

His answer was the one she'd hardly dared hope for. And not in the least what she'd expected. She didn't know *what* she'd expected, exactly. But it certainly wasn't a quick, firm "yes."

However, he *had* said it. He was willing to marry her.

Everything was working out, after all. And she should be happy. She should accept his answer and go on from here. After all, when a non-marrying man said he would marry you, the last thing you should do was question his decision.

But she couldn't help it. She *did* question his decision.

She cleared her throat. "Aaron, I have to ask. Are you sure you want to do that?"

He gave her a puzzled frown. "Didn't I just say yes?"

"Well, yes. You did. But, well, you know how you are."

He looked at her sideways. "And that is?"

"You told me from the first that we weren't going to be married."

He made a low, amused noise in his throat. "Under the circumstances, I've changed my mind."

"Ah. Well."

The look of amusement faded. "Well, what?"

"Well, that's good. But—"

He put up a hand. "Why not just leave it right there, with 'that's good'?"

"Because, now that I think about it, maybe you should take a little time, not rush into this. I'd like you to be certain that marrying me is what you want to do."

"Celia. You asked. I answered. I think we've about covered it."

"Well, I want you to have a little time to—"

"I don't need time."

She swallowed. "You don't?"

"No." He looked at her probingly. "Do you?"

"Well, of course I don't. This is what I want. To marry you. To have our baby..."

"Okay then." He stood. "We're in agreement." He came toward her.

She watched him, feeling edgy. Wary.

Oh, what was the matter with her? She'd gotten exactly what she wanted.

Why didn't she feel better about it?

He held out his hand. "Come on." After a slight hesitation, she put hers in it. His grip was warm. Firm. The familiar thrill shivered through her, the excitement when he touched her. Her inconvenient apprehensions faded a little.

He gave a tug and she was in his arms.

Oh, it did feel good to be there. She sighed and rested her head against his chest.

"Look at me." He took her chin and tipped her face up so that she had no choice but to meet his eyes. "I think you'll make a fine wife. I've always thought so. Whether I'll make much of a husband remains to be seen. But I'm willing to give it a try— for you. And for the baby."

She told herself she was content. They would do the best they could with the hand they'd been dealt. "About the wedding…"

"I'll leave that to you. I suppose it ought to be soon, don't you think?"

"Yes, I agree."

"And this *is* Las Vegas. Pick a chapel. Any chapel."

"Well, actually…"

He brushed a kiss between her brows. "I'm listening."

"I was thinking we might get married in New Venice. Something small and simple. Next weekend, if I can get everyone together. Just family and close friends.''

"However you want it, that's fine with me."

She reconsidered the time frame. If they married next Saturday, that only gave her five days. No way it would be enough time. "On second thought, maybe the weekend after next."

"Whatever you say."

"You are certainly agreeable."

"You don't like me agreeable?"

"Well, I just want to be sure that—"

He cut her off by laying a shushing finger, so lightly, against her lips. "Celia. I'll tell you what you can do."

"What? Anything. Please. Just say it."

"You can kiss me."

"Kiss you? I'd love to, you know that. But that's not what I—"

"Celia."

"What?"

"Shut up and kiss me. Will you do that?"

"Oh, I do worry, you know, that you—"

"Shh."

She groaned and shut her mouth.

"Kiss me. Come on…"

She tipped her head back and presented her lips.

"That's better," he said, and brought his mouth down on hers.

They ended up in her bed, of course. And after that, she called Casa D'Oro and ordered them lunch. He had some work he needed to catch up on, so he left her at a little after three.

As soon as he was out the door, she called Jane.

Jane said, "Hello."

And Celia said, "I'm pregnant."

"Oh, no."

"Oh, yes."

"Celia Louise, what is the matter with you? I assumed you had sense enough to always practice safe sex."

"I did, I *do*—well, *almost* always."

"*Almost* isn't good enough, and I think you know it isn't."

"Janey. Please. I know I screwed up. A lecture is the last thing I need right now."

"You're right," said Jane in a gentler tone. "Are you okay? Do you need me to fly down there?"

"Thanks for offering. I'm fine—well, as fine as a any woman who went and got herself accidentally pregnant ever is."

"Do you know what you're going to do?"

"Have a baby in about eight and a half months."

"Ah. And when do you plan to tell Aaron about this?"

"I already have."

That actually gave Jane Elliott pause. "Wow. Celia Louise. Good going. You got right on it."

"Yes, I did."

"What did he say?"

"Before or after I asked him to marry me?"

Jane gasped. "You didn't."

"I did."

"Talk about being direct. I'm impressed. I truly am."

"Thank you," Celia said modestly.

"And his answer was?"

"Yes. He said yes."

Jane let out a Jillian-like shriek of pure delight. "Oh, Ceil. I'm so happy for you. I am. Happy and proud. You went out and you got what you wanted. It took you a while to do it, but you did tell the man you loved him right up front, no coyness. No games or denials. And now this. You were right there, right on the case, telling him the truth when you found out you were pregnant. Telling him what you wanted— marriage. And it's all worked out, hasn't it? Because, all along the line, you have told the truth. You have behaved with total honesty and absolute integrity."

Well, more or less, Celia thought, but didn't say. Jane was right—for the most part. Celia *had* been honest, or at least, she'd tried her best to be.

Jane asked, "When's the wedding?"

With a large measure of relief, Celia let the subject of her integrity drop. "Well, that's another thing I called about. We want it to be soon. Saturday after next, if possible. That's the twenty-eighth. Not a big production or anything, just family and close friends. And up home, there in New Venice and—"

"How about here, at my house?"

"Oh, Janey. You read my mind. But are you sure? It *is* short notice, and—"

"I'd love to do it."

They talked for another hour: about the guest list— small enough that Celia would simply call everyone and invite them personally—about the food and the beverages, the cake and the flowers. Jane said she'd contact Reverend Culpepper over at the Community Church and ask him to do the honors. If he wasn't available that particular Saturday, she'd ask her father, the judge.

"You call Jilly, right away," Jane instructed before she hung up.

"I will," Celia promised.

Jane said goodbye and Celia punched the speed-dial for Jillian.

"Ohmigod, pregnant." Jillian groaned. "What will you do?"

"I already did it. I asked him to marry me. And he said yes."

Jillian let out a gleeful cry. "Get *out* of here."

"No. It's true. The wedding's a week from this Saturday. At Jane's."

"Ceil, I gotta hand it to you. You do not fool around."

"So, will you be there?"

"Just let anyone try to keep me away—what about a dress? Have you found one?"

"Hey. I'm fast, but not that fast."

Jillian rattled off the names of three Las Vegas bridal boutiques. "All of them are wonderful. You'll love what they have."

"Thanks, Jilly."

"And if there's anything I can—"

"You know that there is."

"I figured as much. What?"

"Janey's got the list. She'll call you."

"All right. Ceil?"

"Hm?"

"Are you happy?"

"Ecstatic."

And she was, she kept telling herself, as she called her mother and her two sisters and three brothers. She was marrying the man that she loved. Of course, she was happy.

Celia's mother was her usual distracted self. "Celia. Wait a minute. Oh, it's so hard to keep track of all you kids these days…"

"What, Mom?"

"Well, it's just that I didn't know there was anything going on between you and your boss."

"We haven't been…together, as a couple, for all that long."

"Oh, honey. *Aaron Bravo?* I know you love your job, but—"

"The point is, I love *him.*"

"Oh. Well. If that's the case, then what can I say?"

"Congratulations?"

"Well, yes. That. And, Celia dear, you do have to realize, it is a shock. You, marrying one of those Bravo boys…."

Patience, thought Celia. "Mom. As I said before, I love him. And I'm marrying him."

"Hmm," said her mother. "Hmm…" Celia waited. Finally, her mother admitted grudgingly, "Well, I *have* heard that those boys have done well for themselves."

"That's right. They have."

"But that Caitlin is a wild one still. One man after

another and each one of them younger than the one before. I don't understand how she—''

"Will you come to my wedding, Mom?''

"You know your father and I hate to fly. All the inconvenience, and then, who *knows* what could happen these days? The world is not what it used to be and—''

"Mom. Will you come to my wedding?''

Her mother heaved a huge sigh. "Oh, well, I suppose it's one of those things we really shouldn't miss.''

"That's right.''

"Okay. We'll be there.''

After her mother, Celia called her oldest sister, Annie.

"Aaron Bravo?'' Annie said, as if maybe she'd heard wrong. "Celia, are you *serious?*''

"Well, no, Annie,'' Celia replied. "This is all a big joke. Are you laughing yet?''

Annie backpedaled madly. "Look. Celia. I'm sorry. It just surprised me, that's all. I know you work for him and everything, and I know he's made it big and all. But *I* went to high school with the guy. And he's one of those bad Bravos and…well, I don't know. My sweet, shy little sister *marrying* him? Who would have thought that would ever happen?''

"It's happening.''

"You're mad at me.''

"No. Honestly. I'm not. Can you come to my wedding?''

"Saturday, the twenty-eighth, you said?''

"That's it. It's in New Venice.'' Annie and her

husband John and their two kids lived in Susanville, California, now. "At Jane's. You remember Jane?"

"Of course I remember Jane."

"Great. Well, she lives on Green Street now, in the house that used to belong to her Aunt Sophie."

"I remember that house."

"The wedding will be there."

"Right. The twenty-eighth."

"At two in the afternoon."

"I'm going to say yes now. I can't think of anything that would keep us from it."

"Thanks, Annie. I know you guys are busy and this is short notice."

"Celia. I have to ask."

Celia didn't like the sound of her sister's voice. "Yes? What?"

"Well, he isn't in the Mafia or anything, is he? I think I heard somewhere that—"

"Annie. Please. Do you honestly believe I'd marry some Wise Guy?"

"Well, what do I know? I live in *Susanville*."

"Annie. Listen. Aaron's not in the Mafia. I swear to you."

"Well, good. Sorry. I had to ask."

After Annie, Celia called the rest of her siblings, leaving messages for Peter and Katie, reaching Tom and Janice. Tom said he'd be there. Jannie said she'd try.

And what about Caitlin? Celia found herself wondering once her own family had been called. What about Cade and Will Bravo? They should be called, too. She'd told Aaron she'd take care of inviting everyone. But really, he should be the one to tell his family he was getting married.

She asked him about it that evening, over dinner, at his place. He said, "Sure, I'll call my brothers. But do you think that maybe you could call Caitlin?"

"Aaron. She's *your* mother."

"Don't rub it in."

"Oh, very funny."

He waved a hand. "Okay, okay. I'll call her. First thing in the morning. How's that?"

She knew she should leave it alone then, let him call his mother and say whatever he wanted to say to her. But guilt was eating at her, gnawing away. She really should have told him about those private conversations she'd had with Caitlin, the one concerning how Caitlin so thoroughly approved of Aaron and Celia as a couple, the one about wedding bells and baby carriages. In fact, if she had any backbone at all, she would just go ahead and tell him right now.

But she didn't.

What she said was, "Do you plan to tell her about the baby when you call her?"

He set down his fork and reached for his wine. "I don't know. I hadn't thought about it." He sipped. "She's going to find out eventually, right?"

"Yes, you're right. Of course, she will."

He set his glass down. "Celia. Whatever's on your mind, I wish you'd just say it."

"Well, the truth is, I'd rather you didn't tell her I'm pregnant yet. I told Jane and Jillian, but I don't really want anyone else to know right now. Let's get married and get into the rest of it later."

"Fine. Works for me."

If only she didn't feel so guilty, so much like a conniving, scheming lowdown cheater. "Aaron, I've been thinking. What about a prenuptial agreement?"

He set down his fork again. "What? You're afraid I'm after your money?" He was grinning, of course. He thought he was so funny.

"Oh, stop it. You know what I mean."

The grin turned to a frown. "Celia, I have to say it. You're acting strangely."

"I'm not. I'm trying to be fair. Here you are marrying me because I slipped up and got pregnant. There should be a prenuptial agreement, one that makes it very clear I can't take you to the cleaners. I mean, you know, if it doesn't work out."

He slid his napkin in at the side of his plate, poured himself a little more wine and sat back in his plush, high-backed chair. "Tell me. Do you intend to take me to the cleaners—if it doesn't work out?"

"Well, of course not."

He stared at her over the rim of his glass. Then he set the glass down. "Don't you think I know that? Don't you think I know *you?*"

"Well, of course, but—"

"Listen."

"Uh. All right."

"Maybe I don't know a lot about marriage. Maybe I've never seen a good one up close. Maybe marriage is not a place I ever intended to go. However, given the circumstances, I *am* going there. But don't kid yourself. I would *not* go there under *any* circumstances with a woman I didn't trust absolutely. Only an idiot would do that. And I'm no idiot.''

He trusted her, absolutely.

Now, why did that make her want to burst into tears?

She set her own napkin by her plate and then reached out, hesitantly, touching the sleeve of the silver-gray cashmere sweater he wore. "Oh, Aaron," she whispered. "What a beautiful thing to say."

He put his hand over hers. "Forget the prenup idea."

"All right. If you're sure."

He pushed back the big chair and rose to his feet, pulling her with him, taking her mouth in a long, slow, sweet kiss. "Let's go to bed," he suggested, when at last he raised his head. "We're always in complete agreement there."

He kept his word about calling Caitlin. He did it first thing Monday morning, in his office.

Celia knew he did because five minutes after he disappeared behind his door, her line rang. She picked it up and said, "Aaron Bravo's office."

And Caitlin said, "Good job, baby doll."

Celia experienced that urge again—the one that made her want to scream rude things and slam down the phone.

"Sweet cakes, you there?"

"I'm here."

"I have to hand it to you, you got it done faster than I ever expected."

"Well, Caitlin. I honestly do not know what to say."

"Oh, don't get a nasty tone with me. You know I'm on your side. You've got to be knocked up, right?"

"Knocked up. What a lovely way to put it."

"Answer the question."

Celia grimly kept her mouth shut.

Caitlin didn't seem particularly bothered by her lack of response. "I'm gonna be a grandma. Hmm. Am I ready for that? You know, I think I am. I surely do."

"Well, that's a load off my mind."

"Hah. So I *am* right about this."

Celia gave up. "All right. Yes, I am pregnant. But I did not intend to be. It was carelessness, that's all."

Caitlin chuckled. "Hey. What does it matter how it happened? Do you hear me complainin'?"

"I know that you think I tricked Aaron into this."

"Uh-uh. Don't you even imagine you can see inside my head. The point is, I'm happy about it. Very happy. I'm lookin' forward to the wedding, to havin' you for a daughter-in-law and to bein' a grandma at last."

Now, *there* was an image. Caitlin Bravo, a grandma—her own baby's grandma. Celia shivered at the thought.

"Sweetie pie." Caitlin's whiskey voice was all coaxing softness. "Don't be mad at me, now. You and I both know all I did was give you a few little shoves in the right direction."

"Caitlin, it was an *accident.*"

"Whoa, darlin' girl, no need to shout."

"I am not shouting." Was she? She cast a guilty glance at Aaron's shut door.

"You eat right, you hear? No booze."

Could this be happening? Prenatal advice from Caitlin Bravo—who had married a kidnapping murderer and just recently ended a passionate liaison with a Fabio look-alike half her age?

"Don't let Aaron work you too hard. And if you need me, you just holler."

The line to Aaron's office blinked—saved by the red light. "Caitlin, I have to go."

"Sweetheart, wait." There was a plaintive note in that smoky voice. "You're not *too* mad at me, are you?"

Celia wasn't, not really. The person she was angry at was herself. "No, Caitlin. Of course not."

"I'll be good to you. My *son* will be good to you."

"I know that."

"See you at the wedding."

"Yes. See you there."

Celia punched the button that put Aaron on the line. "Yes, Aaron. What can I do for you?"

"I like the way you say that."

His teasing tone warmed her. She chided, sweetly, "Not in the office."

"Such integrity. It amazes me."

Integrity, she thought. There it is, again. My favorite word.

"Ready?" he asked. It was time to go over the calendar.

"I'm on my way."

* * *

Celia found her wedding dress the next day, on her lunch hour. It was knee-length and sleeveless, of ivory silk, tiny pearls embroidered at hem and neckline. A little hat went with it, complete with a small froth of veil. It was perfect for a low-key, friends-and-family-only afternoon wedding.

Jane called that day and on Wednesday, Thursday and Friday, as well, to report on her progress with the wedding preparations. Reverend Culpepper would preside over the ceremony. The cake had been ordered. The flowers were handled.

Celia had decided to forgo attendants. She and Aaron would simply stand before the reverend and say their vows. She wrote checks to the bakery and the caterer, the florist and the party supply store. It was all going smoothly—or so Celia kept telling herself.

Aaron treated her with tenderness and passion—and patience, when she couldn't help asking if he was *sure* this was what he wanted.

"I'm sure," he would say, a little more wearily each time.

Each time she asked him, she knew that she shouldn't have. That he'd answered the question over and over and if his reply didn't satisfy her, asking again wouldn't help.

But in the back of her mind, guilt went on nagging. Everyone thought she was so honest, so chock full of integrity—and yet she'd lied to herself from the first in this relationship. She'd always wanted more than he wanted to give.

And she never had told him the truth about Caitlin.

She felt as if, somehow, by not telling Aaron of his mother's schemes, she had colluded with Caitlin. After all, in the end, what Caitlin had suggested had come to pass.

On Friday night, five days after Celia had proposed and Aaron had accepted, they went to his rooms for the evening. He'd had dinner sent up. It was waiting in the dining room.

He pulled back her chair for her. She saw the blue velvet jeweler's box just before she sat down. She knew by the size and shape of it what it had to be.

And right then, at the sight of that little blue box, she understood what she had to do.

He was still waiting behind her. He moved up close and whispered in her ear. "Open it."

She could feel him, feel the warmth and solidness of him so close. She wanted to press herself back against him, to turn in his arms and offer her mouth to him—to put off what she now knew was the inevitable.

"Open it," he said again.

And the moment of cowardice passed.

She picked up the box. Her hand wasn't even trembling. She lifted the lid.

It was as she'd expected.

An engagement ring. A platinum band and a huge square-cut diamond flanked on either side by a matched pair of slightly smaller triangle-shaped stones.

"Do you like it?"

Like it? It took her breath away.

And at the same time, she was thinking, *Diamonds. It always ends in diamonds....*

Her heart contracted.

Oh, she did love him. And he was a much better man than a lot of people realized, a man determined, no matter what, to do the right thing, to make the best of the situation he'd found himself in.

The ring sparkled, winking at her as it caught and reflected the light from the chandelier above the table.

It always ends in diamonds....

That wasn't his intention now, of course. She knew very well he'd never given any other woman a diamond *ring* when he said goodbye to her.

But then, in this case, he wasn't the one saying goodbye.

He put his hands on her shoulders, so gently. Oh, his touch was magic. How would she live without it?

"Celia." His voice was teasing. "Say something."

She turned in his arms, met those blue, blue eyes. "It's absolutely beautiful. And I can't accept it."

Chapter Fifteen

Aaron took her meaning.

Or at least, he thought he did.

But then again, maybe not. Who could say what Celia really meant lately?

He asked warily, "You don't like it?"

Those slightly slanted hazel eyes were dewy with unshed tears. "Aaron. I love it." She snapped the box shut. "But I—"

He put up a hand. "You know, you say that word a lot lately. *But* this, *but* that."

"I know. I'm sorry."

"Don't be. Just stop."

"I can't."

"Sure, you can."

"Aaron. Please. It's not going to work."

"It," he repeated, as if he didn't know what "it" was.

"This," she insisted. "Us. You know what I mean. It's not right. Not fair to you."

"Don't you think I should be the judge of what's fair to me?"

"No, not in this case."

"Why not?"

"Because you're only trying to do what's right."

"And that's wrong?"

"No. No, of course not. *You* have done nothing wrong. Nothing at all. It's *me,* don't you see? I can't *do* this. You said from the first that you didn't want marriage. And that hasn't changed. You just feel you *have* to marry me now."

He backed off a step. And he kept his arms at his sides. It was difficult not to reach for her, not to grab her and shake her until she said something that made a little damn sense.

"Thank you, Celia," he muttered, low. "Now I know how I feel."

"Oh, please don't be sarcastic."

He strove to keep his tone level and reasonable. "You were the one who brought up marriage in the first place. *You* asked *me* to marry you."

"Yes, I did. And I shouldn't have. It was a mistake, a…throwback reaction involving faulty logic. I thought, I love Aaron and I'm pregnant with his baby, therefore it follows that we should get married."

"Seems like sound enough logic to me."

"But it's not. Not necessarily. Not in our case."

"Why not?"

She pursed up her sweet mouth at him. "Oh, for about a thousand reasons."

"And those reasons are?"

"Well, first of all, the basic one. You don't love me."

Love.

He supposed he should have known that was coming. And hell, what was he holding back for? He was willing to take a chance on marriage with her, wasn't he? If he was going to go that far, why not go for broke? "Look, Celia. I—"

She was shaking her head. "No. Please. That's not what I want. Truly, it's not. Your saying something you don't mean isn't going to fix anything. My point is, this baby inside my body is making me face a few things I've never wanted to think too hard about before. And one of those things is, well, it's about what I really *am,* as a person, you know?"

He didn't. So he waited. He figured she'd go on.

She did. "What I am, Aaron, is *ordinary.*"

"Ordinary."

"Yes. I am. Oh, I can wear bright clothes and dye my hair red and sleep with the glamorous, sexy, brilliant CEO of a Vegas super-casino. But at heart, I'm a small-town girl, a little shy, a middle child from a big middle-class family, a middle child who never got enough attention, but who still knows her mother loves her, still feels a bond with her sisters and her brothers."

It was nice to learn that she thought of him as glamorous, sexy and brilliant. But where was she going with this? What was the point here? "I'm not following. Because you're a small-town girl from a big family, you can't marry me?"

"That's right."

"I don't—"

She cut him off. "Aaron, I slept with two men before you and I—"

Where the hell did that come from? "Wait. Slow down. Back up."

"What?"

"Are you about to tell me there's some other guy in the picture now?"

She stiffened. "Are you crazy? I love *you*."

"Then these other men you're talking about are strictly past tense?"

"Well, of course they are."

"Then Celia, why are you talking about them?"

She gave a desperate cry. "Because I'm trying to *explain* myself to you."

"Ah," he said, for lack of anything better. She was doing a truly terrible job of it, but he saw no percentage in pointing that out to her.

"Will you *let* me explain?"

"Absolutely. Please go on."

"All right. I'll try." She blew out her cheeks in a frustrated breath. "What I'm getting at is, those guys were nice, ordinary guys."

"Okay…"

"They were nice, ordinary guys and they said that they loved me and wanted to marry me."

"I see." He didn't. But it seemed the right thing to say.

"I told them no." She waved the ring box at him,

shook her head. "Both of my best friends married early. And got it wrong. But not me. I was *different*. Oh, I thought I was so special, that I was secretly meant for great things. But now, I'm realizing the truth. And the truth is, I didn't marry those other guys because I didn't love them. I didn't find love until you. And now I've found you, well, I want the things that any ordinary woman would want. I want you to be my devoted husband. I want our baby. I want us to make a home...."

He almost asked her why the hell she hadn't noticed that he was perfectly willing to give her what she wanted.

But he didn't. He didn't think it would do any good.

And then she said, "And also, well, I feel like a rotten, lowdown cheat all the time now and I hate feeling like that."

He forgot all about the big questions, the ones that centered on the nature of love and whether Celia Tuttle was or was not ordinary at heart. "You feel like a cheat. Why?"

She blinked. He knew then that he was onto something. Finally. "I just, well, there are things I should have told you that I didn't tell you and—"

"What things?"

"Oh, Aaron." She held out the velvet box. "Please. Just take this back. Take it back now." She pushed the box at him.

And that did it, somehow—her shoving his ring at him as if she couldn't wait to get rid of it.

Really, was there any reason to keep on with this?

If she wanted to break it off with him, fine. Let her have what she wanted. He was damn good at a lot of things, but dealing with the complex emotional needs of women wasn't one of them. He'd accepted that about himself early on, taken care to make it clear to all the women he dated that love and marriage and baby carriages were not part of the deal.

But then along came sweet Celia Tuttle, a nice girl from his hometown, the best damn secretary/personal assistant he'd ever had the good fortune to come across. He still didn't know quite how she'd done it. But she'd slipped under his defenses, awakened things inside him he hadn't even known were there. She'd made him start thinking that maybe, with her, things could be different.

He saw now how wrong he'd been.

And come on. Who said the baby meant they *had* to be married? Maybe this was a case of him thinking way too much like the ordinary guy Celia seemed so certain he wasn't. Why not approach the situation differently, why not think outside the box a little here? He could still make arrangements to take care of both her and their child, whether Celia was his wife or not.

He asked her one more time. "You're sure? This is what you want?"

She nodded, her lips pressed tightly together, unshed tears glittering in those pleading eyes.

What else could he do? He extended his hand. She set the small blue box in it. "All right. What things haven't you told me?"

She swallowed. And her gaze shifted away. "Now this is settled, I don't think we really need to—"

"I think we do. What things?"

"Aaron, I'd like a little time. I'd like to go home, for a few days, to New Venice, and I—"

"Fine. Do whatever the hell you want to do."

"Okay, I'll—" She started to turn.

He caught her arm. "Not yet."

"Aaron—"

"What things?"

"Let go of me."

He held on tighter. "You have some talking to do and you know it."

"Let go."

He held on and he waited.

And she gave in. "All right, all right. Fine. I'll tell you."

He loosened his grip on her arm. "Talk."

She pulled away, tried one more time to put him off. "Aaron…"

"*Now,* Celia."

"I…"

He waited. He would wait forever if he had to. But he'd get to the bottom of this before he let her leave that room.

The phone on the long table against the far wall chose that moment to start ringing. Celia stiffened at the sound and looked at him hopefully.

"Don't worry," he said, schooling his voice to a parody of tenderness. "I'm not going to answer it."

"Bu—"

He put up a hand. "Do not say that word."

She swallowed, looked away, then reluctantly back

at him. They waited for the ringing to stop. When it did, the room seemed preternaturally silent.

"Talk," he said. "Now."

And at last, in a small voice, she confessed, "It's about Caitlin."

He swore under his breath. "I should have known. What did she do?"

"Oh, Aaron…"

"Quit stalling. Give it up. You owe me this much, Celia. You know that you do."

"But if we—"

That did it.

He threw the box with the ring in it, threw it good and hard—aimed it an antique mirror on the wall several feet away and let it fly. The mirror cracked. The box flew open. He didn't see where it landed—or if the ring was still in it when it did. He didn't see and he didn't care.

Celia had fallen silent. When he looked at her again, she was watching him in wide-eyed shock. He was sorry he had frightened her. But the swift, violent action had achieved its intended result. She'd shut her mouth over the damned evasions.

With deliberate care, he moved away from her, around the curve of the oval table, to the place that had been set for him. Pulling out his chair, he sat, leaning back, ordering his body to relax, making it clear to her that he presented no threat.

And he didn't—as long as she told him what he wanted to know. "What about Caitlin?"

Celia had moved behind her own chair. He hid a

bleak smile. Did she imagine that chair could provide any kind of real barrier, if he wanted to get to her?

He asked again, "What about Caitlin?"

She cleared her throat. "Well, your mother just…from the first, from that weekend of your birthday, when she caught us in the back hall of the Highgrade together, she started in on me."

"Started in on you, how?"

"She said she knew there was…an attraction between us. And she was in favor of it. She said she was 'betting on me' in this 'game.' That was what she called what you and I had together, our love affair—a game." Her soft mouth quivered. He thought of how he was never going to kiss that mouth again.

He didn't like thinking that, so he ordered his mind *not* to think it. "What else?"

"Um, then later—you remember that day she came here and then just went home without seeing you?"

"I remember. What about it?"

"Well, the truth is, you weren't the one she wanted to talk to."

His mother's odd behavior that day had nagged at him. Now he understood. "She came to see *you*."

Celia nodded. "She told me she'd heard we were lovers and that she approved of it. She asked when the wedding was going to be. I told her what I thought she already should have known—I mean, since you *are* her son, she has to be aware of how you feel about marriage."

"You explained that we weren't getting married."

"Yes, I did. And that was when she said I should…'do what I had to do,' I think was how she put it, to get a ring on my finger. She hinted that I should get pregnant to force your hand.''

''And did you?'' he asked, though he already knew the answer.

''No!'' she cried. ''I didn't. I swear.''

''Well, then. Why are you beating yourself up over this? My mother is my mother. You grew up in New Venice. You know what she is.''

''But I...I didn't *tell* you. And I *should* have told you. But I was too *ashamed* to tell you. Because I *did* want to marry you. I wanted to marry you right from that first day I figured out that I loved you. Your mother was right about that much.''

She was clutching the back of the chair now, as if she needed it for support. She lifted a hand and swiped at her eyes, dashing the traitorous tears away. ''I'm just...well, everybody keeps saying I have so much integrity. That I'm so honest and up-front and truthful all the time. But as you can see now, I'm not. Not at all...'' She gripped the chair again, in both hands, hard enough that her knuckles grew pale. ''I'm just so confused. I need some time, I really do, to try to sort all this out in my mind....''

Aaron felt a powerful urge right then, to rise and go to her, to comfort her. But he knew she didn't want that—not from him anyway.

Her choice, after all, had been made.

He stayed where he was and told her gently, ''It's all right. Take some time off. However long you need.''

She was shaking her head. ''You have to see. It

really isn't going to work, for me to try to keep my job with you."

He supposed she had a point. "I understand. I'll find someone else. And I'll make financial arrangements for the baby."

Tears welled in her eyes again. "Thank you."

"I *will* want to see the baby. To be a part of his life."

"Yes. I know. I would never try to stop you from—"

It was enough for now. "Fine. We can work all that out later."

"Yes. Of course. That's good."

He stood. "Come on. I'll take you to your rooms."

She stepped back. "No. It's all right. I can get there on my own."

"You're certain?"

"Yes." She raked a hand through that silky red hair. "And listen, I don't want to leave you holding the ball on this. If you need me to stay a while, to find my replacement and—"

"No. I'll worry about that."

"Oh, Aaron. Are you sure?"

"Positive." He approached her slowly. She allowed it, though her eyes warned him not to touch her. He dared to put his hand at the small of her back. He felt her shiver and stiffen, but she didn't jerk away. "At least let me walk you to the elevator."

She gave him a brave and slightly wobbly smile. "All right."

They left the dining room, went down a short hall to the entryway with its round etched-glass skylight overhead. He pressed the button that summoned the elevator.

Seconds later, the door slid wide. The night elevator operator tipped his hat at them. "Mr. Bravo. Ms. Tuttle."

Aaron nodded and Celia did the same. She stepped into the car.

"Goodnight, Celia."

"Goodnight, Aaron."

The door slid shut and she was gone.

Chapter Sixteen

When she got back to her rooms, Celia went online and booked a flight home. Then she called Jane.

"The wedding's off."

"Oh, no."

"Oh, yes. I broke it off. I couldn't go through with it. I broke it off—and then I quit my job."

Jane must have known it wasn't the time to ask questions. "Come home. Stay with me for a while. Get your bearings."

"God. I was hoping you'd say that. That's all I want right now, to come home. I've got my plane ticket. But I wasn't quite sure where to go after I got off the plane. I was thinking I'd book a room at the New Venice Inn."

"My house," said Jane. "That's where you're staying."

"It's crazy, isn't it? All I want is to go home to New Venice, but no one in my family lives there anymore."

"I'm here."

"I know. And I'm so glad."

"Shall I pick you up in—"

"No. I'll rent a car."

"I don't mind coming for you, Ceil."

"I can get there on my own, and I'd prefer it that way."

"Well, all right. Just come straight to the house. If I'm not here, I'll be at the store."

"Jane."

"Hmm?"

"Please don't call Jillian. I'll do it, tomorrow. She's going to tell me I'm nuts. Maybe I *am* nuts. But I don't think I can bear to hear about it tonight."

"Whatever you say. Just come on home."

When Celia pulled up in front of the house on Green Street late the next morning Jane was there, waiting for her. Celia heard the screen door slam and then her friend was racing down the steps toward her, dark hair flying.

Celia popped the trunk latch and got out of the car.

Jane had her arms out. Celia went into them, hugging back as hard as she could, burying her face in the fragrant cloud of curly hair.

Finally, Jane took her by the shoulders and held her at arm's length. "It's good you're here."

"Yeah. Yeah, it is."

"Let's get your things."

They went around to the trunk. Jane pushed up the lid and grabbed the heaviest of Celia's three bags. Celia took the two smaller ones. They started up the walk, Jane in the lead.

They were halfway to the steps when Celia noticed the man standing in the shadows of the porch next door. He was tall and lean, in faded Levis and a dark shirt, lounging against a post, watching them: Cade Bravo. He nodded when she looked his way, one side of his mouth lifting in a slow half-smile.

Like Aaron, she thought. Not Aaron's smile exactly, but close....

Her heart felt too big, suddenly, to fit in her chest. It ached to be squeezed in so tight.

She realized she was lagging, and hustled to catch up.

Once inside, she turned to Jane and spoke in a carefully neutral tone. "I see Cade Bravo's come home at last."

Jane made a low noise of agreement—then changed the subject, which was just fine with Celia. "The blue room is waiting." Of Jane's various spare bedrooms, the blue room was Celia's favorite.

Jane led the way up the stairs and into the cozy room with its white-quilted twin beds and blue window treatments. She set the suitcase she was carrying on the nubby-textured blue rug. "I should get back to the store."

"No problem. I'll put my stuff away, get settled in."

"You're sure you don't mind if I leave you all alone?"

"Janey, I'm okay."

"I'll be home by six or so."

"No hurry. I'll be fine."

Saturday afternoon, sitting in Jane's kitchen at the round oak breakfast table, Celia used her cell phone to call the wedding guests—except for the Bravos. She'd leave that to Aaron, however he wanted to handle it.

Was that cowardice on her part? Probably. But it seemed presumptuous, somehow, to take it upon herself to call his family with this particular news. Add to that the fact that his family included Caitlin and, well, Celia simply could not face the prospect of talking to that woman right then.

It didn't take long to make the calls. Everyone was so understanding. They spoke to her quietly. With sympathy. They asked, "Are you all right?"

She gave the appropriate responses, she thought. She said she regretted how things had worked out, but she really did feel that it was for the best.

She didn't mention the baby.

Time enough for that later.

She called Jillian last, told her what had happened, that the wedding was off and she was staying at Jane's.

Jillian said just what Celia had expected her to say.

"Celia Louise, have you lost your mind?"

"Jilly—"

"I do not believe this. Tell me you didn't say it. Tell me I've heard you all wrong."

"I couldn't go through with it. It's that simple. He never wanted to marry me and—"

"Oh, please. As if Aaron Bravo is some babe in the woods. That man is no pushover. No woman would ever get him to do a thing he didn't want to do. If he agreed to marry you, he *wants* to marry you. The question is, why did you screw it up?"

"Jilly, I really don't want to talk about it."

"But you *need* to talk about it. You know that you do."

"No. I don't. Maybe eventually, but not right now."

Jillian sighed. "For the sweetest and shyest among us, you certainly can be stubborn as a bad-tempered mule."

"I have to go."

"No, you don't. You just don't want to hear what I'm telling you. You've made a big mistake and I want to know why and you just don't want to think about it."

"I have to go. I mean it."

"Okay, okay. Take care of yourself. Please."

"I will."

"Guess who came into the bookstore today?" Jane asked that night at dinner.

Celia shrugged. "Haven't a clue."

Her friend's dark eyes gleamed with teasing humor. "I'll give you a hint. Fabio meets the Terminator."

"Hans is back."

"It would appear so."

"Back with Caitlin?"

"Can't say for sure, yet. But ask me in a day or two. By then, the gossip mill will be churning. I'll have the whole lurid story."

For some insane reason, Celia felt defensive for Caitlin. "Why does it have to be lurid? They *are* both adults. Maybe she just *likes* him. Maybe *he* likes *her*."

Jane frowned. "Ceil. Hey. I have no axe to grind here. Sincerely, I don't. It was an attempt at conversation, you know? A little humor—or so I thought."

Celia did know. "Sorry. I'm out of line. And not a whole lot of fun to have around, either." She gave her friend a rueful smile.

"It's okay," Jane said gently.

Celia cut another bite of chicken. When she looked up from her plate, Jane was watching her. "What?"

Jane picked up her water glass and took a thoughtful sip. "Well, maybe if you let yourself talk about it…"

Celia groaned. "Janey, I don't want to talk about it. I don't want to scheme or plan. I don't want to figure out my next move. I *have* no next move. I honestly don't."

"Did I suggest that you scheme or plan or figure out your next move?"

"No. No, you didn't. I'm sorry…"

"Stop apologizing. I just want to understand what *happened*."

"I broke it off. I felt like a liar and cheat and I—"

Jane let out an outraged cry. "Well, that's just ridiculous. You are no cheat."

"Oh, don't defend me. Please. I did what I did and it's over now. I just want to rest a little, eat your wonderful food and take shameless advantage of your hospitality for a few days. Then I'll start thinking about finding another job."

"But you *love* him."

"Yes, I do. But it didn't work out."

"Celia—"

"Jane. Please. Can we leave it alone?"

They watched a video and turned in early.

Celia didn't sleep well. She lay in the narrow bed, staring at the blue walls, thinking of Aaron, missing him, telling herself she'd done the right thing.

And wondering why it all felt so wrong, why she couldn't stop Jillian's words from echoing in her head.

If he agreed to marry you, he wants *to marry you. The question is, why did you screw it up?*

Aaron wasn't sleeping well, either. He found he was angry and getting angrier.

He was angry at Celia, who had got what she said she wanted: him. And then decided she didn't want him, after all.

And even more than at Celia, he was mad at his mother, who never could seem to keep herself from barging in and messing up what would most likely have worked out just fine if only she'd had the common decency to leave it alone.

But she hadn't left it alone. And now Celia was gone.

He would have to get over her.

And he would. He'd get over her. He'd take care of business, get on with his life.

Last night, after Celia left him, he'd returned to the dining room and found the ring—on the floor, beneath a sideboard. It was undamaged. The box was there, too, a few feet from the ring. He put the ring in the box and put the box in his private safe.

Monday, he'd return it. He'd also see about getting the mirror he'd broken replaced. He'd see about replacing Celia, as well—professionally, anyway. The idea of taking another lover right then made him feel vaguely sick to his stomach.

And *that* made him angry all over again.

He told himself things would be back to normal soon. He told himself to forget it.

Forget Celia. Forget Caitlin. Forget both of them—for a while, anyway. Just put them completely out of his mind.

And the thought of doing that made him even madder.

Because he couldn't forget them, not really. One of them had given him life.

The other not only carried his baby—she'd also managed somehow to make off with his heart.

Chapter Seventeen

The Silver Unicorn Bookstore was closed on Sunday. Jane stayed home, with Celia. It was a gorgeous spring day, crisp in the early morning, turning warmer as noon approached. At around eleven, Jane suggested they sit out on the porch. They brewed a pot of peppermint tea and took it outside with them.

Jane got comfortable on the porch swing. Celia took the teak rocker with the needlepoint cushion. She closed her eyes and rocked slowly and told herself to appreciate the beauty of the day, to forget her problems for right now. There would be plenty of time to deal with them later.

But then she heard brakes squealing. She opened her eyes in time to see the gleaming black Trans Am come barreling around the corner from State Street.

The car screeched to a stop at the curb, right behind Celia's rented Chevy Corsica.

Caitlin.

So much for forgetting her problems.

Aaron's mother emerged from the low black muscle car, her raven hair big and hard and shining, her black jeans way too tight. Today, her shirt was black satin and her spangles dayglow green. Her scarf was green, too, tied at the side of her neck, the ends flowing jauntily along her shoulder. She slammed her door good and hard, hustled around the front of the car and marched up Jane's front walk.

At the base of the steps, she planted her feet wide apart and propped her fists on her hips. "Cade said you were over here—and that Aaron wasn't. I didn't believe it."

It appeared that Aaron had failed to call his family and let them know there would be no wedding, after all.

Jane stood from the porch swing. "Caitlin, why don't we all go inside and—"

Rising herself, Celia cut in. "It's okay, Jane. I'll handle this." Jane sighed and sat back down. Celia turned to Aaron's mother once more. "Believe it," she said. "We've decided not to get married, after all. The wedding is off."

"What?"

"Caitlin, you're shouting."

"Damn right, I'm shouting. And who is this 'we'? My boy decided the wedding was off? My boy said he wouldn't marry you?"

Celia turned for the front door. "That's all I have to tell you, Caitlin. Please go away."

"Wait. You get back out here. You get back out here now."

Celia pulled open the screen and pushed the front door inward. She crossed the threshold, shutting the door silently behind her.

Caitlin called Aaron at a little after noon.

"I just paid a visit to Jane Elliott's. Your woman was there. She told me the wedding was off. Is that true?"

He should have hung up on her. But he found himself imagining the great pleasure it would give him to wrap his hands around her neck and squeeze until her false eyelashes popped off.

"Aaron. Damn you, darlin', are you there?"

"Ma," he warned softly. "The last thing you want right now is my undivided attention."

She kept on shouting. "Aaron, you get home. You work things out with that sweet little girl. You hear me? Am I getting through?"

She was. "If I come home, Ma, I'll be looking for you first."

"Fine. Come on. You just come on. You think I can't deal with you? You try me, darlin' boy. I am ready for you, in spades, and that's a fact."

"All right, Ma," he said very quietly. "I'm on my way."

Aaron flew the Cessna. He arranged to have a rental car waiting when he touched down at the Comstock Valley airstrip.

He pulled into the parking lot behind the Highgrade at ten past four in the afternoon. A minute later, he was striding through the back hall, shouting his mother's name.

She was waiting in the bar for him, standing in front of the first pool table, arms folded across her chest. There were a couple of regulars there, bellies up to the bar—and Bertha behind it.

The Viking boyfriend was back. Hans stood well behind Caitlin, between the two pool tables, holding a pool cue and looking formidable, ready to rescue his aging lady love if it came to that.

"Out," Aaron said. "All of you."

The regulars drained their shot glasses and made themselves scarce. Bertha flipped up the hinged section of counter at the far end of the bar and slipped into the back room.

Hans stayed where he was.

"You, too, big guy. Get lost."

The Viking laid the pool cue on the table in front of him and folded his massive arms over his gigantic chest, so his pose was a mirror of Caitlin's. "I vill stay."

Caitlin shot him a look over her shoulder. "Go on, Hans. I can deal with this on my own."

"I said, I vill stay."

"Hans. I am fine. This is between Aaron and me. Please go."

Hans didn't move.

"Terrific," said Aaron. He was maybe three feet

from the bar. No effort at all to bend over and grab a stool.

"Aaron..." his mother warned.

She got no further. Aaron smashed the stool across the bar. The bar withstood the blow. But the stool broke apart. Aaron was left holding one of the legs. "Hans. This is private. Will you please get the hell out?"

"I despise violence and I don't vhant to hurt you," said Hans. "Don't make me."

Caitlin had already turned and was on her way around the pool table on the far side. "Hans. I mean it. This is none of your business and I want you to—"

Aaron threw the stool leg—not very hard. It hit Hans lightly in the chest and bounced to the floor.

Hans's chiseled Nordic features turned the color of an overripe tomato.

"Come on, then," said Aaron wearily, waving his hands in a come-and-get-me motion. "Let's go. Let's do it now."

"Hans!" shouted Caitlin.

But it was no good. Hans lowered his head and rushed, bull-like, at Aaron.

Aaron waited until the other man was almost upon him, then he leapt for the bar, sliding across it, swinging his legs over and landing behind it in one unbroken move.

It took Hans a moment to realize that his target had relocated. He staggered to a stop. "Huh?" And then he spotted Aaron. He threw back his huge blond head and let out what could only be called a battle cry. Then he dove for the bar.

Aaron was waiting for him with a fifth of Jose Cuervo Especial raised high. Hans hit the bar and Aaron hit Hans on the top of the head. The bottle shattered, sending shards of glass and good tequila flying everywhere.

"Ugh," said Hans. He looked at Aaron, his expression soulful. "Daht *hurt*." And then, with a groan, he collapsed across the bar.

Caitlin started swearing. She rushed to the Viking, who groaned some more and slowly raised his head again.

"Oh, sweetheart," Caitlin cried. "You okay?"

"Huh? Vhat?"

Caitlin wrapped her arms around Hans and sent her son a fulminating glare. "Let me take him in the back."

"Great. Go. Now."

"Come on, now. It's all right. Come on with me...." Caitlin led Hans around the pieces of broken stool, past the pool tables and through the door to the storeroom, leaving Aaron alone in the bar with glass in his hair and tequila all over his black leather blazer—not to mention the polo shirt beneath it. He brushed at the mess, wondering what the hell was the matter with him, anyway.

He never should have come here.

And he certainly shouldn't have taken his frustrations with Caitlin out on poor Hans, who'd done nothing in the least offensive—well, beyond falling for Caitlin in the first place, and then insisting on defending her. He wondered with a kind of bone-deep weariness when his mother would finally consider herself old enough to give up getting involved with inappropriate men.

Guilt started nagging at him. He looked around at the mess he'd made and decided he ought to at least clean it up. So he got the broom and dustpan from behind the bar and swept up the glass, then wiped up the booze that had spilled on the counter, and mopped up what had made it to the floor. After that, he went around by the pool table and picked up the pieces of the stool he had destroyed, setting them on one of the tables, ready to carry to the Dumpster out back.

When things were in reasonable order again, he sat down at the bar. Not two minutes later, the door to the back room opened. Caitlin came through it alone.

He rose from the barstool. "Is he okay?"

"Fine," she said tightly. "No thanks to you." She strutted toward him in those high-heeled boots of hers, stopping about a foot away, resting an elbow on the bar and slinging out a hip, in her best don't-you-mess-with-me stance. "All right. Go ahead. Lay it on me. Do your worst."

Aaron opened his mouth. And then closed it without making a sound.

He'd thought he had a lot to say to her.

But somewhere between smacking a stool across the bar and whacking poor Hans with a full tequila bottle, the whole trip home had begun to seem ridiculous, an exercise in futility, an excuse for breaking up the furniture and getting in a fight.

And now what?

The usual. He would shout at her. She would shout back at him.

It would just be the same-old, same-old, what they'd done all his life. Hotheaded Caitlin Bravo and one of her boys, going at it, shouting the house down.

He muttered, "What in hell is the point?" And he started to turn.

"Aaron. Wait."

Something in his mother's voice stopped him—something without pretense. Something raw and true and freighted with pain.

He turned. Even in the dim bar light, he saw the change that had come over her face. She looked older, very tired—and infinitely sad.

"Aaron. I only want the best for you. You know that, don't you?"

He grunted, shook his head. But when he spoke, it was gently. "Yeah. Yeah, I know that."

"I saw you two together, you and Celia, that night of your birthday, and I knew it. I knew she was the one for you. That in spite of everything, of all of it— your father, who never was any kind of father at all— and the way I raised you that never gave you much of anything to go by. In spite of yourself, and your determination not to let anyone get too close to your heart. In spite of all of that, you had found what matters, anyway. I didn't want you to blow it."

He considered her words, then shook his head again. "I don't think I did, Ma. I think you blew it for me."

"Oh." Her red mouth trembled. "Did I? Really? Are you sure?"

"Damn it, Ma. Don't start bawling on me. I don't think I can take that right now."

She sniffed, swiped her nose with the heel of her hand. "Yeah. You're right. Cryin' is a weak woman's trick." She smoothed those too-tight pants of hers. Then she sucked in a big breath, yanked her shoulders back and stood up tall. "I'm tougher than that."

He almost smiled. "You are. Tough as nails. There's no one tougher."

She put a boot up on the stool between them and leaned on the bar again. Then, uncharacteristically hesitant, she asked, "Celia was the one who called the wedding off?"

"Yeah."

"Did you...tell her you love her?"

"I started to. She stopped me."

Caitlin frowned. "And you let her do that?"

He stuck his hands in the pockets of his jacket, gave her a long, cold look. "Don't judge me. You weren't there."

Those false eyelashes swept down. She appeared to be studying the toe of her high-heeled boot, the one hooked over the rail of the stool.

He got tired of waiting for her to say whatever it was she had on her mind. "All right, Ma. Spit it out, whatever it is."

Her head came up and those black eyes were focused on him again. "I just think you ought to be lookin' at your own part in this."

"And that is?"

"Well, darlin' boy. You let her chase you until she

caught you. And you never really let her know for certain that you *wanted* to be caught. So she let you go. You say I blew it for you. Maybe I did. But only because you let it happen.''

Chapter Eighteen

A few minutes later, Aaron came out the back door of the Highgrade carrying the pieces of the barstool he had broken. He stopped at the Dumpster and tossed the pieces in. Then he turned for his rental car.

But he never got inside. About a foot from the driver's door, he found himself pausing, turning his head up toward the clear blue spring sky. He had an urge to walk.

He went around the side of the building and then down the alley between the Highgrade and Jane Elliott's bookstore. In seconds, he was emerging onto Main.

The old hometown looked good, he thought, as he started up the street. The trees were leafing out and the sidewalks were clean and someone had slapped a new coat of paint on Garber's Hardware Store.

He reached State Street in no time. And he turned onto it. It was right then, at that corner, that he realized where he was going—up to Green and to the right and then four houses down, to the Victorian with the cream-colored fish-scale shingles up under the eaves and the terra-cotta shiplap, with the green and red trim and the cute little tower tucked into the front porch.

He mounted the steps and rang the bell.

The heavy oak door had beveled glass in the top of it. After a moment, Jane Elliott appeared. She saw him through the glass and her dark brows drew together.

At first, he was certain she would turn away and leave him standing there.

But then she pulled the door wide. She didn't, however, unlatch the screen.

She moved up close, rested a hand on the doorframe. "Yes, Aaron?" she said in a low voice, but briskly. Her nostrils flared—must have got a whiff of the Cuervo all over his jacket and the front of his shirt. But she didn't let the fact that he smelled like the inside of a bottle throw her. "What can I do for you?"

"Is Celia here?"

She sent a furtive glance over her shoulder. "I…"

"She *is* here. Right?"

Jane faced him squarely again. "Yes. Of course, she's here. She's resting."

He longed to tear the screen wide, shove poor Jane aside, and go pounding up the stairs, shouting Celia's name. He asked, carefully, "Could you ask her if she'll speak with me?"

"Look, Aaron. I don't know if—"

Right then, they both heard the sound of footsteps on the stairs. He looked toward the sound and so did Jane.

"Jane. Who is—" Halfway down, she saw him. She froze, her hand on the railing. Her eyes were huge, her face so pale. That mouth he'd thought he might never kiss again formed a soft, startled *O*. "Aaron…"

He thought, I have to talk with you. *Please….*

But somehow, the words stayed trapped inside. And beyond whispering his name, she wasn't talking, either.

Jane broke the silence. "Listen. Aaron. Why don't you come in?"

He managed an answer, though he did not take his eyes off Celia. "Thank you. I will."

Jane unlatched the screen, pushed it wide. He ordered his legs to move. And then he was inside, standing by the door in Jane Elliott's entry hall, staring like a long-gone fool at Celia, who stared back at him, motionless, from the stairs.

Another silence descended. It didn't bother Aaron in the least. He was here, with Celia. He could *see* her. She was real. For the moment, it was all he needed.

All he could handle.

All he could possibly take.

Eventually, Jane said, "Look. If you two don't mind, I think I'll just leave you on your own for a little while. I have a few things I keep putting off over at the bookstore. You know how it is. There's always some little project or other just crying out to be done.'' She waited for one of them to say something.

Neither of them did.

Finally, Jane was forced to try again. ''Celia? Is that okay with you? Do you mind if I go?''

Celia kind of shook herself. ''Yeah, Jane. Great. See you later.''

Jane grabbed a purse from a narrow table against the wall. ''Back in an hour or so.'' She went out the front door.

Time hung suspended. Aaron didn't mind. He was here and she was here and that was very, very good.

After an eon or so, Celia started moving again, coming toward him down the stairs.

Aaron drank in every line, every curve. She wore no makeup and her hair was smashed flat on one side. She had on a pair of gray sweatpants and a baggy Cal State Sacramento T-shirt. Her feet were bare.

She stole his breath and stopped his heart.

When she got to the bottom of the staircase, she stopped, her hand on the newel post. *Come on,* he was thinking. *Don't stop there.*

She must have read his mind. Her bare feet brushed the gleaming hardwood floor as she came toward him again.

At last, she was standing right in front of him.

She sniffed. Frowned. ''Aaron? What is that smell?''

He hung his head. ''Tequila.''

She reached out a hesitant hand, touched the still-damp front of his shirt. His heart turned over in his chest. He wanted to grab that hand, hold on tight, never let go. At the same time, he didn't dare move.

He confessed, still staring at the floor, at her beautiful bare feet. "I stopped by the Highgrade before I came here. There was a little altercation. I broke a bottle of tequila over Hans's head and got it all over myself in the process."

"Oh, Aaron…"

He jerked his head up and looked in her eyes again, searching hungrily for clues to her true state of mind. He wasn't sure what he saw. She looked…disappointed. Yes, that was probably it. Disappointed in him.

He hated himself. "I have no excuse for what I did. I was angry. I took it out on poor Hans…."

"Angry at me?"

"Yeah. And at Caitlin."

Her soft fingers brushed his jaw, stroked back into his hair. God. He did love that. The feel of her hand in his hair.

"Your mother does love you. Very, very much."

"I know. But her love is damned hard to take sometimes."

He thought he saw a tiny smile twitching at the corners of that tender mouth. But then it was gone. She ran her finger down the side of his neck, making his pulse race and his body burn. "You don't seem angry now."

He couldn't stop himself. He caught her fingers, kissed the tips of them, one by one. "Celia…"

"Oh," she said. "Oh, Aaron…" She pulled her hand free and stared up at him. What the hell was she thinking? If only he knew.

She seemed troubled. Or maybe anxious. "I have some things to say to you."

His pulse thudded hard in sudden dread. "What things?"

"Well, I've been thinking, the past two days…"

"Yeah?"

She turned from him. It took all the will he possessed not to reach out and grab her. She went to the stairs and sat on the bottom step, drawing her legs up, wrapping her arms around them, then shyly patting the empty spot beside her. "Sit by me?"

He approached with caution. She looked up at him, anxious—yes, he was sure of that now. She was anxious. He didn't know why she thought she had to be anxious.

They were working it out, weren't they? That was why he was here.

But then again, maybe she'd decided *she* didn't want *him*. Maybe that was what she'd been thinking about these past two days.

Maybe— No. Better not do that, not jump to any conclusions about what was happening here. Better to wait. See what she had to say.

He turned and dropped down next to her. "All right. What?"

She gathered her legs in closer, rested her sweet soft chin on her knees. "Well, my friend Jillian said something. When I told her the wedding was off. She asked me if I was crazy. I was expecting that—I mean, because she knows how I love you.''

His heart soared. She still loved him!

And she was still talking. ''Also, Jilly knows about the baby. Naturally, she'd question why I would break it off with you. But she said something more. She said that you weren't the kind of man who would let himself get roped into doing something he didn't want to do. That you never would have agreed to marry me unless you *wanted* to marry me.''

''I hardly know this Jillian. But I like her. A lot.''

She laid her cheek on her knees and looked at him wistfully. ''You mean, she's right?''

Words were lost to him again. But he managed a nod.

''Ah,'' she said. Did she look happy? He wanted to think so. She lifted her head, faced forward again and stared off into the middle distance. ''Jillian said I needed to ask myself why I would break it off with you, when marriage was obviously what *both* of us wanted. She said I should ask myself why I would want to screw up what we had together.''

He leaned into her, just a little, brushing against her, then pulling back. ''And *did* you? Ask yourself?''

''Yes, Aaron, I did.''

''And did you come up with an answer?''

''I think so.''

''And was it, maybe, that you had chased me and caught me and asked me to marry you? And you wanted more from me than the lukewarm yes I gave you?''

She turned her head his way again and blinked at him, owl-like. "How did you figure that out?"

"My mother does have her moments."

She drew back a fraction. "Caitlin told you that?"

"She did."

"Well," she said, looking surprised and pleased. "What do you know?"

Did she lean toward him? Or did he make the first move?

He couldn't have said. He only knew that they were leaning toward each other. And then, at last, their lips were meeting.

They kissed for a long time, sitting there on the bottom stair, neither quite daring to reach out with their hands yet, each craning toward the other, mouths fused but otherwise not touching.

At last they pulled apart—but not too far. Only a few inches.

And he said, "I love you, Celia Tuttle. You are everything I didn't know I was looking for. I think we can have a terrific life together. Please, please, will you marry me?"

She didn't answer. Not in words. But those hazel eyes were shining and her mouth was softly parted.

That mouth was too much of an invitation to resist. So he kissed her again, this time pulling her into his arms. She kissed him back. With all the sweetness and passion he'd learned to love in her.

She turned in his arms, sighing, and ended up stretched across his lap. He lifted his head and she opened lazy eyes, raising a hand to stroke his hair at the temple. "Did you hire my replacement yet?"

''There is no one who could replace you, and you know it.''

''Good. I like my job. We'll have to make some changes. Later. But not right away.''

He said gruffly, ''I suppose you'll want to get a house, stop living at High Sierra, now we're having a family.''

She shook that mussed red head. ''No. I like where we live. And our baby will be fine there. Maybe eventually, we'll have to get a house like regular folks. But not for a while…''

He wondered at the musing look on her face. ''What are you thinking?''

''Oh, about being ordinary.''

''*You* said that. I didn't.''

''Aaron. It's okay with me. There's nothing at all wrong with being ordinary.''

How could he disagree? If Celia was ordinary, then ordinary was just what he'd needed all his life.

''Okay,'' he whispered. ''You are incredibly, fascinatingly, enchantingly *ordinary*.''

She beamed up at him. ''Thank you—and I was also thinking about Caitlin. And you…''

''What about Caitlin—and me?''

''I was thinking that Caitlin is big and bold and sloppy and loud. And you are so fastidious at heart.''

He grunted. ''I reek of tequila. I just beat up my mother's boyfriend. That's fastidious?''

''You've been frustrated lately.''

''Yes, I have.''

''But at heart, you are a fastidious man. I think you grew up wanting some order in your life. And you got it by keeping love out. I've made things a little bit messy for you."

He thought about that for a moment. Then he nodded. "Maybe you have. But I'm not complaining—and Celia, you know you haven't said yes yet."

"That's right. But I will."

He bent close again—and kissed her nose. "That's good to hear."

"Where's my ring?"

"In my safe at High Sierra."

"Will you let me have it, after all, when we get home?"

"You know that I will."

"Funny..."

"What?"

"This is one time in your life when diamonds will be the beginning and not the end. And right now, it occurs to me, I want to rethink the wedding...."

This information did not surprise him. "However you want it, that's how it will be."

"Now I'm thinking we should have it in Vegas. At High Sierra."

"That's doable."

"And I want to invite your cousin Jonas and his wife...."

He swore under his breath.

She chuckled. "*I* will invite them. You won't have to do anything but be nice to them if they agree to come."

"You are relentless."

"Well, yes." She looked much too pleased with herself. "I guess I am."

"Say yes to my proposal. And mean it. Say yes now."

"Yes, Aaron. I will marry you."

"Say you love me."

"Oh, I do. I love you with all my heart."

"Now kiss me."

And she did, pulling his head down and parting her lips with a tender, eager sigh. Aaron gathered her in and returned her kiss—passionately, fully, without reservation.

A non-marrying man? Not anymore. Aaron Bravo had the only woman for him held close in his arms.

And he was never, ever letting go.

* * * * *

Don't forget to look out for Cade's story in
Mercury Rising *by Christine Rimmer.*
On sale in October 2003.

▼ SILHOUETTE®
SPECIAL EDITION™

AVAILABLE FROM 15TH AUGUST 2003

THE HEART BENEATH Lindsay McKenna
Morgan's Mercenaries

As Lieutenant Wes James and Lieutenant Callie Evans raced to save victims in an earthquake-ravaged city, past pain kept Wes from surrendering his heart. But he ached to make Callie his...

MAC'S BEDSIDE MANNER Marie Ferrarella
Blair Memorial

Dr Harrison MacKenzie wasn't used to women resisting him—but feisty nurse Jolene DeLuca's flashing green eyes told him to keep away. He was captivated...but could he convince her to trust him?

HER BACHELOR CHALLENGE
Cathy Gillen Thacker
The Deveraux Legacy

Businesswoman Bridgett Owens wanted to settle down—but irresistible bachelor Chase Deveraux was not the sort of man she wanted to marry. Until a passionate encounter changed everything...

THE COYOTE'S CRY Jackie Merritt
The Coltons

Falling for off-limits beauty Jenna Elliot was Bram Colton's worst nightmare—and ultimate fantasy. But now that she was sharing his home, he couldn't ignore the intense passion between them...

THE BOSS'S BABY BARGAIN Karen Sandler

Lucas Taylor only married his secretary Allie so that he'd be able to adopt a child—but a night of passion resulted in pregnancy. Could he overcome his past and keep the love he'd always longed for?

HIS ARCH ENEMY'S DAUGHTER Crystal Green
Kane's Crossing

Rebellious Ashlyn Spencer was the daughter of Sam Reno's worst enemy...yet she melted Sam's defences. Could the brooding sheriff forget her family's crimes and think of a future with her?